DIMITRI BORTNIKOV is a Russian-born French writer. Born in Samara in 1968, he had a rather eventful youth: after his medical studies were interrupted by the then-mandatory military service in the Soviet Army and later by the fall of the Soviet Union, he worked as a nurse, a librarian and a dance teacher before leaving Russia to join the French Foreign Legion (for a short while) and finally settling in Paris, where he worked as a cook for an old Russian countess.

His first novel, *Syndrom Fritza* (The Fritz Syndrom), was published by Limbus Press, Saint Petersburg, in 2002 and was a finalist for the Russian Booker Prize and the National Bestseller Award.

Bortnikov wrote two more novels in Russian, *Svinobourg* and *Spiaschaya Krasavitsa* (Sleeping Beauty), and in 2008 published his first work written in French, a novella entitled *Furioso*.

In 2011, Editions Allia, Paris, published Bortnikov's first novel written in French, *Repas de morts*, unanimously saluted by the critics.

In 2017, Bortnikov wrote a second novel in French, the epic *Face au Styx* (Facing the Styx), which was awarded the Best French Novel of the Year Prize of *Lire Magazine*.

Betimes Books are proud to publish *Repas de morts* in English as *Soul Catcher*. This is the first English translation of a work by an outstanding writer whose literary career to date is impressive and whose future is undoubtedly full of promise.

Since 1999, Dimitri Bortnikov has been living in Paris, where he is a full-time writer.

SOUL CATCHER is a partly autobiographical work narrated by Dim, a Russian exile living in France. In prose that is as harsh as it is poetic, the narrator reminisces about his childhood, his family, his dead loved ones, his lost love, and the country in which he grew up, as well as talking about his life in France, the country of his voluntary exile.

Vivid, dreamlike images and the author's own thoughts and lucid observations are conjured up by Bortnikov's unique rhythmic, syncopated language that is truly his own, intense and mesmerising. The result is a daring, powerful novel like no other, which captivates readers with the power of his writing and stays with them long after reading.

The importance of this work, which is his first full-length novel written in a language that is not his mother tongue, lies in his original voice, which critics often compare to Céline, Calaferte, Beckett, or Joyce.

Praise for *Soul Catcher*

"A modern *Inferno.*" —*Les Inrocks*

"… A poetic and visceral survival guide, of which each sentence, each word, each dot even, adds a star to the heavenly vault we all carry in ourselves. […] Dazzlingly inventive." —*Le Télérama*

"This sublime text has rhythmic power, incantatory energy, insolent humour."
—*Le Monde*

"In the tradition of Céline, Calaferte and Jauffret, Bortnikov signs a literary objet that is truly disconcerting, carried by a bitter, syncopated language that devours everything along the way. […] Iconoclastic." —*Lire Magazine*

"Better than a novel, a long feverish blues full of ghosts, sorrows and hungry dogs. We get lost, we drown, and we don't care…" —*Le Nouvel Observateur*

"A masterpiece. It happens sometimes that a text, from the first sentence, puts you into a state of astonishment that will not leave you until the end and convinces you that you are reading one of those major works of fiction that will mark you forever." —*TechnikArt*

"This strange novel – partly autobiographical – is built as a succession of reminiscences and dreamlike images of the steppe, the tundra and Paris. But no matter what the story is – what matters here is the power of his writing, harsh and infused with venomous poetry." —*L'Express*

"Here is an animist prosopopoeia. Here is an ardent work." —Tristan Felix

"Bortnikov's audacity verges on genius. A constant verbal insurrection." —*Gonzai*

"Powerful, paroxysmal, his prose doesn't resemble anyone else's." —*Livres Hebdo*

"Language plays a crucial role there, with that breathless rhythm that follows the narrator's hallucinated thoughts." —*Euranet.eu*

"With its breath-taking prose and its tenebrous beauty, *Repas de morts* is a literary uppercut. Radical, exhilarating, a joy of reading of a rare intensity."
—*Transfuge*

Soul Catcher

DIMITRI BORTNIKOV

Translated from the French by Svetlana Pironko,
in collaboration with Dimitri Bortnikov

BETIMES BOOKS

First published in the English language in Dublin, Ireland, in 2020
by Betimes Books CLG

www.betimesbooks.com

Originally published in French as *Repas de morts* by Éditions Allia in 2011

Cet ouvrage a bénéficié du soutien du Programme d'aide à la publication de l'Institut français

Avec le soutien de l'Ambassade de France en Irlande

Supported by the Embassy of France in Ireland

ISBN 978-1-9161565-2-4

Cover image © Grégory Morizeau, with his gracious permission

Cover design by JT Lindroos

Table of Contents

I

I was masturbating when my father phoned. I was too spent to get up and turn down the volume of the porn movie. There was that dog, joyful as a young bear, and a woman who was greedily lapping up his sperm. It was going on and on and the dog was shuddering, a big smile on his face… The woman spoke German then French. Then she lay down, her legs spread impossibly wide, and she was laughing and patting the belly of the bear-dog… And the dog was melancholically lapping her steamy wound… And that's when my father phoned.

It was the second time since my mother died – that he called me I mean. And just then… they started to sing! There, on the screen! Two guys, two women and the bear-dog. Before it was the usual dirty talk in French, Baise-moi… Baise-moi comme une chienne… Prends ça… Oh ohhhh baise-moi… And then… they started to sing.

I was listening to my father breathe then talk then try to find the words. To fail… In the end he couldn't talk anymore. He was just breathing. Breathing deeper and deeper. He was going down and down, lower and lower, lower than the ground… he wanted to follow his wife down there.

He was exhaling night my father. It was night where he was. The deepest night. Night like under the ground and he… he was exhaling pain.

I'm not crazy, not at all. Suddenly I heard my father sing. Sing! Very quietly he was humming. Not crazy, me, no. I did hear my father sing.

On the screen, they were singing, the three whores and their hunks… And my father… I was listening to my father sing in the phone.

It was night. There was beeep beeep beeep in the phone. He must have hung up. Beeep beeep… I must have been listening to them for a while. But the singing went on and on. There, on the screen, they couldn't stop themselves from singing.

I was sitting there. I remember that long night well, very well.

I could hear from the screen No love! No love. Baise-moi! Bouffe-moi! The women, they were whispering so quietly and then louder… Alone they are alone. No men no fathers no brothers no sons. Singing… That contagious singing. That killer singing… They were singing with their eyes closed. Alone we are alone… No love!

They were screaming ah ah ah! No love… Ooooh… cold so cold… They were singing the cold. When the cold is forever. When all you can do is sing – No love.

I find myself sitting in the middle of the night. It's everywhere, the night. I have never had such a long night. That was everywhere. In the pockets of my blue jeans, before me and behind. Under my feet under my nails in my hair. The roots of the night in the seeds of my hair. That night… I drowned in it.

It calmed me. I was calm. Calm… No more souls to catch. You reach the bottom of things. So slowly. You go down. So gently you touch the bottom. When you envy the dead. The seeds of their hair that sleep in the deep ground... I wanted to cover the mirror. With a piece of fabric... the tradition. And to turn my back to it.

Yes, everything. He told me everything on the phone. She fell in the street. She stayed on the ground all night. All night on the ground. ---She must have slipped---She was so frail in the end... Do you hear me?---Hey?---Are you there?---Talk to me---Say something...---I can't hear you!---

Yes, I could hear him. I was there. He was calling me from his home. From his quiet hell. He went quiet himself. We didn't talk too much. We went empty. Not even a breath, no echo, nothing.

Life left me in peace. I slipped off its hands. And it took pity on me.

Life... It sings us lullabies and. It falls asleep itself. You can see the heart of sadness. I say – now it's over. She's buried. She's in the cold ground. It's cold down there, cold. I'll take a plane. I have money, yes. I was saving. For the dark days. A plane then. That's right. The air is so open and so humble and then the wings... It's good to have wings. To soar... Soar. It will be a long trip. Long. Slow enough to forget it all.

I'm looking at the night... It's endless. It's repeating itself again and again on a loop. It's tied with a slip-knot.

I see my father. Alone he is alone... I see him getting drunk. I see him tearing his shirt. Rrrrrip! He tears it slowly... And then drunk he lies down in the street. Lies down in the dust... His eyes closed he grabs dust and pours it on his chest. Eyes closed... On his face... He wants to go into the ground. To bury himself and. To go along with her, his wife.

I see the sky go by. Hours and minutes. Dust on his face. A mask. He can't cry anymore. He can't die anymore. I see his head in my arms. So heavy… So small. The knot of suffering unties itself ever so slowly. He wanted to drown in the earth. And the earth… It spat him back.

The life of a lonely old man is a pencil with a broken lead. A woman – she knows how to go on.

A man slides down faster than a woman. His slope is steeper. A man is made of small stones… In the end it's run-down and then it's just remnants. Scattered remnants. A woman – no. A woman lives like a cat. Life after life after life.

November, yes, that was it. Imagine the cold and – falling on the ground. In the street, not in the jungle, no, not on the North Pole but in the middle of a street – falling. In a small town – falling. In a town where every dog knows you. Falling and. Staying like this all night.

She was walking slowly slowly always wrapped up looking left and right a thousand times before crossing the street. So frail so alone. The days of old age don't bend anymore… So hard to bend. Harder and harder. But easy, easy. It's over now. Now it's all over. Now it's all dry. Go easy… Go. Letter by letter… Lash by lash. Sound by sound.

Thwack! Thwack! My mother is chopping a rabbit. A female rabbit. We have guests. Swoosh! Swoosh! The bones are singing. My mother is good with an axe. She breaks them bones – like matches. We took out our best plates. With patterns. Blood splashes on me. Hop! I'm the fastest. And the bones are singing.

I see us. My mother with her axe. Her hands covered in blood. Her hands… She washes them six times a day but tonight they will still smell of blood. She's going to wash them with bleach… but I know they will smell of blood tonight. All night. Dinner and all. Yes it's quiet. When my mother's hands smell of blood. I'm used to it. I can sleep peacefully. The smell of blood on her hands. That evening… It is immense that evening and the sunset and our garden.

Our guests. Women children their toys noises of spoons the gurgling of the small sips of the wind jingle jangles of glasses… There is room for all of it. The evening will swallow the people and the sun. Its bed is wide. We'll all lie in it.

My mother and me in the Sunday haze. So serious so idle we were. Before the butchers. Before the Koreans selling spicy grated carrots. Before the farmers. Before the fishmongers with greasy hands. Slippery hands. Before the hands of the butchers' daughters. With their white and red aprons. Very alive yes very alive joyful like seahorses – their hands.

It was their hands, only their hands. Never their faces, I never looked at the faces. I was afraid of faces… They were serious. But there were some that were singing yes, some were singing and I wasn't afraid. I can look calmly at a person who sings. I can be at peace with her face.

At the market I always avoided the faces. I was only looking at hands. People's hands. Thousands hundreds of hands. All sorts of hands. On pigs' cold heads. Fingers on stiff cows' heads. Hands – their name is nobody.

The girls they put them on severed heads of calves. Fingers in their hair-locks. In the clusters of black locks… The calves' severed heads. On trays. Heads of sad monsters.

Those hands and the fingers of their souls. Their name is nobody.

I bow down in fear… To that strength. To that endurance. To that relentlessness. Where does this energy come from? Chasing away flies… Yes, chasing them away from the meat to save the corpses of cows.

They were cursing blinking spinning their arms making holes in the air beating it – chasing away flies and the flies arriving again in clouds. And again. They were talking scratching their backs their necks screaming and falling silent. And so on and on and on… Chasing away flies from the dead fish with its eyes wide open. Away from the heads of cows, the heads of pigs with their eyes shut. Away from mischievous heads. Spitting laughing and spitting again on the ground. Looking at each other and looking at the dogs lapping the pools of meat juices. Rubbing hands and scratching… Yawning slowly and gulping down life. Shuddering. Taking a deep yawn and swallowing the world. Where does this thirst come from? Where from… In each hair in each finger in red hair in grey hair in blonde hair and in black hair… That thirst. Yes.

I was looking at severed sows' heads. Heads with mischievous eyes. With sleepy eyes. I was looking at cows' heads with their huge eyes I was looking at fingers pushing against those severed heads.

I was losing myself and I was losing my mother. I was scared. It was big…

Buffoons with butchered beasts, buffoons with dead beasts. Sad buffoons with beasts' severed heads. I was there… And everything yes everything got into me. The dogs that were licking the blood. The fleas that were sucking the blood of the dogs that were licking the bloodied soil... The thirst... So much life... So much.

The spittle curdling in the dust. The flies that were dipping their palpi in the drops of the meat juices. Flies drunk on blood and heat. Their *bzzzzzz...* That mmmmmm... That lullaby of the market. The crowd of souls. Like a prayer. That mmmmmm... like a temple without a ceiling. And flies in the spittle. Flies receiving the sacraments. Nights are hot. Dogs barking... Shrieks of the trains in the night. Summer... Trains far away.

Doctors' hidden faces. I always recognise their faces under the masks. My mother's eyes and the white around them. I always recognised her behind her mask. The melancholy of white. The smell of white – it helped me recognise my mother. Bleach – I love that smell since then.

In the morning she was helping bring new babies into the world and in the afternoon she was practising abortions. All that... She was helping birth and she was killing...

No time to receive the dead when the new-born were coming and all that, it was too fast, way too fast.

Alone Mother alone. Dead in the street. She had been walking walking. Alone. That horrible winter. Alone... She had been talking all alone – her friends were telling me – it had started that winter. She had been talking to herself. Day after day, alone. A small life... The women told me all that. All the delicious details. They didn't hide anything in their pockets. All... All of it was displayed. And I – I talk to myself too. Out loud – alone. It's my turn to sink. I play opposite my dead mother.

I think of that night. They all came, all, she was on the ground, and then, they all arrived to kill her. Even the aborted ones. Yes – those ones in the first place! Foetuses. They too. Crippled babies. Long-haired babies. Babies with foggy eyes… Thanatos babies… They had been clinging to her for thirty years and then – they succeeded at last.

I know it's the spirits that killed her. The night and the spirits… I know it – they came in numbers, came on purpose and then – it was all over.

They were telling me things. The women. Her friends. Her colleagues. They told me everything. They didn't miss a crumb. No. Inspired! They were carried away! They were whispering in unison. Solo. They know how to whisper sorrows… It can be marvellously whispered solo. Yes. And quietly. No wailing no tears. Silences and whispers… There won't be any mysterious deaths anymore. No solitary deaths, sooner or later they will find you. They will stumble on your dead body. Sooner or later… To tell the story of your death.
Your mother…---You should have seen her---You know, she was roaming the town. Always walking. Always moving---We were bringing her bread milk. Everything---But she was never home---Always out and about---Your mother… As if she was trying to break free---To escape---She was seen all over the place. All day she was roaming---Covered in dust---It was spooky.
---She was wearing… Your clothes… She wears your stuff. Your jumper---Your grey jumper---I don't know if you remember. All torn---You can see everything underneath!---I saw her wandering in town like this---Tell me. Does she think she's a saint?---No I know – she isn't crazy. She had never been crazy I know---

All her girl-friends… They come by, the revenants, those old colleagues. My mother… I see her day after day she's looking for something… She wanders all day. Noon… She was afraid of noon. The hour of the dead. And now she is not afraid anymore. Not afraid of anything. Not noon not the night not the twilight. Nothing. But why that thunderstorm… Why that quiet… She was looking for her death…. Where to lie on the ground… She was looking to lie down. Like an old restless bitch. Smelling the ground. Trying not to fall. My mother… She is roaming roaming. An old lady. She was looking for her Yesterday. Her Yesteryear…

She walks by… I see her walking by. She is looking to get some rest. To take a nap. To sleep and. Dream… Dream… She roams.

Surviving. The worst, we haven't reached it. Not yet. The worst is always to come. The dark days… She was made for taking care of the dead. Death was her boss. Where does that sourness come from? That bitterness? That little smile? She had a lot of patience. And she was waiting for death to come and take care of her. When would she come… She knew how to listen for her steps. She knew how to treat death with respect.
She taught me things. Poverty. Plastic bags. Wrapping up feet. You never get wet. Your feet always dry.

Mama are you crazy? You need shoes!... No no… It will be alright. It's alright for this winter. The rain it stops one day it isn't forever the rain, it will be alright.

But the rain doesn't stop. She'll wear the same shoes next winter, and the one after, and after. Her rain has never stopped. Poverty. Misery. We were gifted for it. To stand up to misery. Straight up… No messing. To look straight ahead. All that to collapse in the end. And the smile… Never forget! Yes, that little smile… It's all coming from her. That grimace of misery, and all the offerings. That rage to bare yourself to the bone.

To operate… Every day – operate. Remove everything. The womb. The ovaries. Every day. Abortions… Removing innards. Sorting them out properly and putting them back in order. Everything. In the darkness of the belly.

Tania. Another colleague, a doctor, another one. "She had been waiting for you. And. One day she understood you wouldn't be coming back anymore. You. You would never come back. She understood it as if it had been announced on the radio. All of a sudden. She understood. She had a ruptured aneurism. Not a word. After that. Nothing. She didn't want to speak. Her life had nothing more to say. No one anymore…"

Tell me, Tania, tell me everything.

She was sacked your mother. Charged with the crime and sacked. Barred. She had helped an old woman to die. That woman was dead for years, yes. Everybody knew that. And us… My God, doctors! All we did was wait. She had asked me too, that old woman. She asked everyone who came to change her nappies. All of us… Really. Everybody knew. She just wanted it to end. We had no painkillers. She was screaming. Screaming! The nurses coming and going, from one scream to another, days, nights another day another night and again and again and always screams… I sang. I don't know about your mother what she was doing not to hear… In the end I was singing. I wasn't talking, I was singing. That poor woman had a son. He didn't want, he didn't want it to last... He was rushing about. Always rushing about. Even in the room where his mother was howling like a bitch he couldn't stop thrashing... He saw me singing. Do something Miss... Give her something, so that she could die, at last, shut her mouth, sleep!

But what could I do? Sing louder, steal painkillers, grab and then inject inject. Inject. When it was calming down – I wouldn't stop singing... We couldn't lull her anymore. None of us... We couldn't. That's how. That's why. And then one day she went to sleep at last. It was your mother who unplugged it all, everything, all that gear. She cut it all. That's how.

They smell of death doctors' hands. The common death. For everyone.

Bleach. Blood. And evenings... They are immense the evenings of that job... Nothing can fill them. Those magician's hands that failed. That's what's inspiring. When magicians fail. When magicians can't do. No one can. That's what's inspiring... When there is a dead body in the room. When death roams the corridors.

Her still hands... Tired, two tired mountains. Old mountains. Low.

Her nails. Childlike faces of the fingers. Those quiet babies. Like dead.

My mother... Her hands smell of blood. Always. Every evening it was the same smell. After the hospital she was coming home late she was walking slowly. She wanted it to go that smell. To go...

Days like sleeping soldiers' faces are all alike. Our soul cleans up after us when we croak.

I see myself by her side, yes I was by her side. We were walking slowly very slowly like those who feel like they left something behind… We were walking and I see myself in a dream yes. In a dream.

We were stopping for a smoke. There were benches under the poplar trees I remember and now there's nothing or maybe a car park. Or maybe not even a car park. Just dust – I'd prefer.

But then… We were in the shade and the wind. It was light and shadow and again light and shadow and no end to it… No end…

She was smoking and me I was listening to the rustling of the foliage. Voices of people I knew but then – they were becoming strange.

Both of us we were getting out of life and. We were very close to it, very close. A lady collapsed on a bench. A lady with hands smelling of blood. A boy by her side. We were quiet then. I liked it. At the exit of life. Life… There is never anyone at the exit.

Flies. No, we weren't alone, they still clouded at that moment – I'm sure of it. I was looking at them landing on us, on my mother's hands. She was so tired – she wasn't even trying to wave them away.

I can still see them, big, like bees. They were clouding around her head. My mother with a crown of flies… Black bees they were walking heavily like blackbirds. I was almost scared of them, those black bees. The bees from hell… The souls aborted that day, it was them. They were landing they were walking on her hands. On those old mountains. I was scared stiff and. I was dreaming. Of those who were thrown into the waters of death and. Who came back as flies to kiss my mother's hands.

She was seeing babies everywhere. Stillborn, aborted. She grabbed my hand once. "I know! I know. They're going to come! They will come. They will say give us your clothes. Us… Look at us! We are naked and we are cold. It's you! You killed us. You. Give us your clothes! And then – They will rip my blouse. My jacket… My jumper… They will rip it all off me! They will shred me! So that I would be like them… With them. Naked. I killed them and now they are saying be like us! You killed us and now – Come down with us! Come with us. Die!"

Her lips were moving… I was dreaming of that too – that she was dead and buried and there under the ground her lips were moving.

The evening was immense. There was room for everything yes everything. Between her fingers the evening was flowing quietly.

My mother's grey hair. Broken strings. Broken threads of life. I see her combing her hair. I see her from a great distance, so great that I think she's playing with her hair. Those strings. She is playing on the strings of her hair. I hear the little music.

Your mother walked – Zoya shows me how. Zoya is another colleague. Her arms… Like a blackbird. Like a blackbird that wants to trick the eyes of an enemy. To divert fate. So that the enemy would pass by pass by… And Zoya shows, Zoya imitates my mother. I see my mother, yes, she imitates her well and I laugh. I want to laugh alone. So are people, they want to show you. To show everything, everything. They really want to. They pour out their guts, it's nothing – I'm used to it. All those guts… But this… the way my mother walked. Zoya has talent. She is so touched by herself, her art, moved even, her eyes are almost pissing. And me I stop laughing, I watch her. When people are moved they show you the knickers of their soul.

And you Zoya – when you are dead… you. Who will show me your agony? Who will impersonate you… The way you walk. Your arms. Who will show me your last days, so lonely. Who will make a farce of your death? Neither bitches nor children. And your life, what is left of it is so long. And who will take you on his back to pull you through your last days. Your departure will be timid Zoya. You will die like a fish, like it's a dormition, like a child you will fall asleep in the middle of the party.

When she was little, she wanted to be a doctor, my mother. She knew the human body and knew how to be close. She knew how to touch it, open it and read it. First her dolls'. Looking at the organs in her dolls and then… The heart is here yes, lungs – they are there. Both. And here, it's the stomach. No, a little lower. It was like showing the way. Showing the way in your native town. The body… She knew it well. Finding your way in the body? Like a cat in a strange house… She could see the illness making its way. Invading the body, this finely tuned thing. She saw people men women becoming nasty from pain. Death was making its way, yes.

She could feel the moment when death was there. That precise moment. How the death of a man an animal a bird makes our life so small and. So immense.

I see her from here, from Paris I still see her eyes… She was looking at death roaming around. Death that was coming anonymously. And her eyes her eyes! She was becoming the eyes that see death coming anonymously. That moment…

And then she's there Death and she takes the name of Nicholas of Paul of Margarita of Elena of Anna...

And I see her old, I see her tired. I'm an old bitch. An old old bitch. A mute bitch. I don't bark anymore. Ah... it's over.

At that time I hadn't seen anyone die yet. Not yet. Our Pushka... The old bitch. The one before Friend. Then him too and the birds... I didn't know how they were ending up in our yard. They must have fallen. They must have been exhausted. Where do they come from the birds when they are getting ready to die? They are there and that's all.

My footsteps frighten them they try to flee. The sound of grass crushed by my feet... The steps of a monster. Heavy steps and the grass blades that bend.

I see myself crouching to watch a pigeon die. I remember one summer people saying – the illness, yes the birds' illness and sheltering their chickens.

I could see pigeons falling from the sky. It wasn't too high their sky, they were flying low and they were falling. On the ground they were motionless and then time was going by – they were waking up... And then they wanted to escape leave fly away... far away somewhere... but they were heavy... They were heavy I could feel it. Before they had been flying somersaulting swirling up in the sky and then – nothing.

I can see myself from here. From Paris, from my rotten room – I see myself crouching and the birds in the grass. I was never telling anyone how they died. I see pigeons from my little room. Fat. Those that walk and those that fly. Their flight is heavy.

I remember yes catching that moment... There, watching pigeons passing away – the moment when they stop moving. Then I was waiting some more. I knew perfectly well that it was over. They would never move again. I was catching that moment. I was staying some more by the little corpse dressed in feathers. I saw them as clothes. I understood – inside it's all over.

The pigeon becomes something else. A thing. It belongs neither to the ground nor to the sky nor to me… And then I was coming back in the evening – and it was even stronger. Stronger and stronger… I was looking but not touching, no I never touched not with a branch not with a stick. If I came back the day after – all was over. It was a sheath of a bird. There wasn't anything anymore. It was grabbed by the ground and. It became ground like everything that is on the ground. Like a stone. Like a stick.
I was catching all that and saying nothing to anyone.
As a child I knew death only from those birds. Then I saw dogs and cats die. People too. But at that time I saw things that were happening in the grass. The ground was too strong too near. I could see low. Low and precisely.

Later I saw other things. Other dead. Death in the farmyard. Death of bigger animals. I had to step back to see them die. Yes. I had to step further away to be with them. To be so small and to see death. So big…

That dog's job… Your mother she was crippled from it. She talks Zoya. Talks… She couldn't sleep anymore your mother. She was saying – I can't bend the tiredness anymore. It unbends. I can't fold my days anymore. They unfold. I have no nights anymore. I have only holes in my diary. Days passing by…

Your mother. She was telling me faraway countries. I can still see her, she would stay up hours and hours…

Standing and looking far away. I think she was looking where you were. Far. Far away. Then she would smile. It's good for my eyes – she would say.
Imagine... She was looking… Far away…

Zoya has a cat. A big cat. He must be incredibly old. He's deaf. I have always known him. Always the same – an old white cloud. He has no name. Cat. She carries him around everywhere in a basket.
He used to almost scare me. That cat climbing out of the basket. Climbing back in and stretching out. All of it in silence. Never miaowing. That couple… Yes. There was something demonic in it. And the other thing. Her teeth. Zoya had beautiful teeth. Teeth and eyes. Pale blue eyes, the eyes of a young girl. When she said hello to me – I had goose bumps. When she took my hand in our dark corridor… That couple had something. Her cat… He would walk past me brushing my feet. He had that habit – to stretch out in my shadow.

You all… My dead. You rush into my head. You've all come.
You grandfather… You sleep quietly. You can, you have been through two wars. In the freezing forests of Finland. First. And then the Great Patriotic War. The greatest. You have drained your cup to the last drop, once and for all. Once back home you would make a baby and go again. In the snowy forests you were killing coming back and making another kid. Going again – and that time it was the Greatest War. The second for you. You were making a baby and then you were killing. There was a balance. Yes, a crazy balance. There you were trying not to arse around you were killing and that was it. No dribbles. At home you

were making your wife pregnant. It went on for four years that war.

Now you are resting, you're dead. Now you can have a break an endless break. You have all the time you need.
He was nice to you Babania. The man who went to two wars. Who killed other men. First the Finns then the Fritz. Back home he would make a baby. Balance…

He spoke little. Ate even less. Drunk not at all. He sang alone. Very quietly he hummed before the fire. Watching it… He would sit down by the stove… Drown, yes drown by the fire. And the flames, he would look at the flames dancing. He hummed… Flames danced wood cracked and you – you sang very quietly. I can see him… Motionless by the fire his face was giving me goose bumps. His face was on fire. It wasn't drunk on war, no, it was sober that face.
He became a spirit little by little. A quiet spirit. A shivering spirit. When I was born he was already far enough down that road. He asked me sometimes to read the Bible to him. The books of the Prophets.

War spirits are cold. He was by the fire, he was singing very quietly, very softly, and I thought he was praying. He was receiving the spirits of the dead. I say to myself – he was asking them to receive him too. Later… Once his cup was drained.
He spoke little. Ate little. Drinking – not at all. Bizarre for a man of the days of old. Watching the fire that yes. That he loved, and singing.

He was gentle, yes – I think. A very gentle person. He made a new doghouse for Friend.

By the fire he watched and watched… His old days in embers. Two wars. The snow hell of Finland. Endless forests… Snow-shrouded… Snipers… Cuckoos hidden in the trees. It was women, yes – once he shot down a cuckoo. Like a bag she falls down… Camouflaged in white. He turned her over and it was a woman. The pale face of a woman. Paleness of a dirty white rag. She was still alive. He saw the face of his mother. His own mother…

She was wheezing that woman. She was wheezing from her lower belly. She muttered something. Then – an arch. An impossible arch… Like when giving birth. Her face twitching she died. Wheezing.

Babania she was telling me all that and he was dead. He was dead her old man. A man who had killed other men… He died too, in his turn. She told me things… At night. She had her eyes open. At night… I asked her why? Why wouldn't she close her eyes! What for… She used to say. Close open. All I see is darkness. It's been years – I see only darkness me…

Him and the fire. Close together. The fire and him. The dance of the fire. The dense heat of the embers…

He was cold for the rest of his life. Fire… His red face was turning black. The evening of that face… The evening of an old man's face. He was a man so he was.

He talked little. He laughed little. He didn't scream at night.

The rest of his days he will pass them by the fire. I see them his hands – gloved with his old skin. Fire… He watches… Watches.

And you Babania… You. My old grandmother. So many people don't know that you're dead. So many people don't even know that you had lived. This is what makes me dizzy.

It never cries a child's happiness… It's we who cry. The love of a child is immense. It is – mountain… But life digs. Digs… In the end it becomes a grave.

I say – those whom I love die. Those who I don't care about live forever.

I was with her. The first five years – always with her. She saw my first teeth. They came afterwards – my father and my mother. One day. They took me back for good. Without a word. Like a bag. I was a bag so I was. They had left me with Babania and then – they came to collect me.

It wasn't that easy. Oh no! I hid myself well! I knew they were coming. I could feel it. One day they will come and that's all! Babania will be finished! I had prepared my hiding place specially… For a few days yes I thought I would have to stay there one two three days! They have to leave me alone! They must go back to where they came from. Let them go back without me! Me – I stay! Here, yes with Babania… With you, Babania… Let them forget me! Let them make another son! Another one! Or a little girl! I'm staying with you… Here. We'll live together. Here. No one. We need no one. A blind old woman and a kid! And so what? I can do anything! I'm your little man. I'm strong… I can carry an almost full bucket of water all by myself. Go away! Babania… They won't take me away from you – no!

And then I hid myself. I hid myself well. I even have bread heels. I had kept them… Yes, at almost every meal. We were concocting them together Babania. You and me! A kid and a blind old woman.

I can see me, me and my father. He found me. He caught my foot! I fought! I was thrashing out! Babania! I was screaming! Miaowing. They grabbed me. In the end… They took me into their arms. I remember it well! It isn't you no! You didn't betray me! I didn't believe them then. Never! It wasn't you who had shown them my hideout... Not you!

I saw... You Babania and then – the sky. You Babania and the sky... Him. From here... what could I bring from here? My eyes... They saw you. They looked at you... A split second... Let it all stop! All! To see her... Let me see her! Let me take something! To bring with me! There... To the city.

He's hurting... The adults thought I was in pain. The poor thing... They wanted to take my heart... They are so good, so fair. They are ready to share the burden. To carry my heart. How heavy it is... Heavy.

Babania... Babania... I was looking looking... I say – my love has no hands. No hands no pockets. Only eyes.

They dragged me to the car. Like a puppy that is thrashing out! Holding me tight! Yes Babania... That's how it was... My new life was beginning... Leaving... no shit no goodbyes! To that city that I hated in advance. The breath of the city will make me dull...

Your stories Babania... Your story of Easter. You were saying – there is a Saviour. You were saying that he was dead. And you were saying – he will come. We were in the abandoned stables. I remember... There was a rat pinned to the ground... A rat crucified with a fork. You didn't see it... I did. I can see us... Even from here – I see us.

You told me... So quietly – he will come the Saviour. Be sure – like you are sure to see this hand. He will come.

I see us again and again. Around Easter. I see the Saviour in the stables. The cold sweat of our Saviour. Those stables... It smells of cold bread. It smells of horses that are gone. Dead... It smells of the night feast when Nyx makes her bread out of dust. And the soul stretches out. It whispers to me in fear.

I would see you only on holidays. Babania… I will get off the bus and I will see you. Alone. You will come alone to fetch me. Blind. You will feel me in the crowd. Blind with tears I will find your arms again. And I will slump. At your feet! I will lie down at your feet. Like our Friend! He will come too later, the dog. He will be there too. I will throw myself into the dust! Babania… Don't leave me please… Don't leave me…

And you – dry eyes. Eyes full of dry tears that made you blind little by little throughout your whole life. You. I was strong, I was growing. I was eating like a horse. I could have taken you into my arms and carried you. Yes, carried you home. You. So dry… So light.

Nights in your house… I can still see those nights. Nights with the radio. You were sleeping… Not me. I was listening. Opera arias. Strange voices… Faraway voices. Strange songs. Very softly very quietly night was singing to me. From far away… The world was becoming too big. Too much… I couldn't get myself to sleep. I wanted to masturbate but I couldn't do it either. Sorrow yes… It was coming from that world… Too big. Too much. It was coming from far away… The sorrow of the night. A child can't hide from it. A child in the night and the world getting too big…

The nights of the first snow. It was falling… Falling… Hiding the little houses. The fields… Our dark river… All night it would snow. And. In the morning – all was white. I would wake up from the whiteness. Everywhere…

Snow Babania… It snows. It falls the same as before. Here in Paris. It snows where you are too. In your lands…

It covers your grave the snow. The grave of your silent man. My mother's grave.

I say – be patient… Snow will cover everything. Our strength, our sorrows… Our trails. Our footprints. Mine – heavy. Yours – so light Babania in that fresh old snow… Softly it will cover our dead. My years to come. It will cover our old age. Our misery. Be patient…

Behind the back of ecstasy – melancholia. Grace Babania. When we are tired we become ourselves. We look far away. Even the blind… Our hands are cats that stretch out coil up curl up into a ball to console us. Babania… I see our farmyard. The beasts they swarm about they scream they cry out sick crippled beasts. Old dogs three-legged pigs cats keeling over roaming about… Wandering souls in a lost railway station. It's the great crossing… Our yard. With her new eyes. She will see everything. There on that island where tired souls go… There, in that yard, where she lived blind. She will return there…

Life… We are only its prints. We don't know how to beg it to touch us again.

Teach me not be scared of the dead. I was whispering to you Babania…
---Tired so I am, my little fox. Half dead half I don't know where---I don't see anything---Years and years like this---Let it take me soon---Let it come for me death---My god I pray – not in winter---Not in winter---Everything becomes heavy---Getting dressed in the morning is a feat---blind---it's no big deal---Groping about---One knows well the clothes of old age---
I was whispering… When you die Babania I will go there. To our mountain. We walked by – you said – there are

things… There… On the top. You forbid me from going there. Solemnly. No questions – you were saying solemnly – no go and that's all. That's it.

You will be dead Babania – and I will climb. Run! Fly up there. At night… I know how… How to sneak away. Nobody could stop me!

She will die in winter. In her sleep. Three days… at home. It was madness. Complete madness. I didn't sleep for three nights. Three days three nights not closing my eyes. I waited for her to wake up. Let her wake up! She was moving… Her lashes! I saw her chest move up… Very slightly move up and down. She's breathing! Wake up Babania! Wake up! I was circling the coffin. Looking. Again… Wake up… Enough Babania! It's not for real… I must have been talking to myself. They thought – he's mad! The parents. They got a fright. Mother told me I had started to stutter! We didn't know what to do. To tie you up? Where? We had Babania dead and you crazy…
She got a fright my mother. They all got a fright. Mad! He's going mad!

Such pain… do you remember – you ripped your shirt, naked you ran away. Gone in a blink! Naked I hid with Friend. Yes in his doghouse. His home. They were looking for me everywhere! They were turning over the snow in the yard! Nothing… Every snowflake – in case I was hiding there. We were together Friend and I… The old dog… My Friend. We were huddled together. Huddled in our sorrow. He smelt good. He smelt so good… My eyes were dry. His too, his eyes were dry.

Beware they were saying. He isn't crying. It's not good. Not good at all. Beware… He should cry. He has to cry this kid!

I fell asleep at Friend's. In his doghouse. His old home. He smelt so good... He was radiating heat. He was radiating life. Strong life. Struggling life.

Once – a fox. I see him as if it was yesterday. A fox skinny like a teenage cat. Trying to swallow a whole chicken. A big one. At once. After, he was throwing up feathers... Babania and I we didn't move. A blind old woman and a child... He was groaning he couldn't regurgitate the feathers. He wasn't afraid. Deaf from the effort. Two steps from him – our Friend the wise old dog half-asleep half-bored, squinting.

I had a dream... To stay with him. There. To live here. In his doghouse. Don't let them find me. Let me disappear... Let them forget me. Why are our eyes dry?! Friend...

I was talking to him... He was wagging his tail. Looking at me. I was talking talking to him... A real sorrow mill I was. I was falling asleep. Waking up, it was daylight. We were warm. Cuddled up. We weren't cold at all.

There is a moment when words die.

Babania dying. Her face... Something is happening... Death closed my eyes with her hand. Something... Her face wasn't there anymore. It had retreated like the sea. I was facing the swamp of life. The tide was low. Low... I saw the bottom.

I was roaming in the snow. Eyes hurting. That whiteness... I was exhausted to death. To throw myself on the ground. To lie down and not to move anymore. Stop. Not a twitch. No more moving.

Something big... I could feel something bigger than me bigger than my body – exploding. Immense. I exploded with no words or screams. I was exploding while walking, while lying down, at school, at home, at the dinner table, at night… I continue to quietly explode.

Now it's another chapter. Now I live like a submarine. I like them a lot. We move in the night… We are blind! We listen and we move forward… Like with you Babania. The deep black. We dissolve in the listening… I love them submarines. Their crews and all. Casting off… The sounds of silence. Slow movements… I took on a few years. I took on water. I am looking for a shore.

That night Babania… How very long it was! Long, cold and blue. I see myself running… In the blue snow running toward the mountain. Our mountain… I remember it all Babania. All. I see my shadow – flying… Under the rare lampposts it and I – two. In the dark I alone. Galloping. Up there…

I see myself running from one sorrow to another. An even bigger sorrow. A sorrow that would bring me down. Trample me. That would rip out my heart. My tongue… My soul mute and at the bottom of the sorrow with no heart or tongue – I would become myself.

Winter. Spring… Summer… We lived in the steppe. I was telling you about death without telling the steppe. I was talking of hibernal agony without talking of the steppe. It's time. The steppe in winter. In summer. It will speak for itself the steppe.

The steppe in winter – agony. In the whiteness – agony. And the steppe in summer is the wait. The long wait. Something… Yes something is coming. Something is approaching. Lining up…

The steppe in winter – frozen agony. White rage. Blood! The steppe calls for blood. The white demands some red. The steppe… Massacres happen in winter. The steppe demands. The man, this warm-blooded shadow looks for blood. Some warmth in the icy whiteness.

I was talking all alone. Falcon, hey falcon! I call it. I see myself there in the steppe. It's noon. You start taking to yourself. Because it's hot. Because the sun has found you. Because the sun is formidable. Formidable… You're talking all alone. But in the steppe you're never alone. At noon the steppe starts spinning. And you, you start talking to the steppe. It penetrates you.

Falcon! Oh my little falcon… Peep… Peep! You call me. A little noon bird. My little blinded falcon… Peep peep it is calling me. Run! Hide quickly! Go into the shade! But there isn't any! You're lost… Lost…
Rage yes. The wisdom of the steppe and. Its fury.
When you come into a dark house… First thing – the dark. Yes. A cave. It blinds you the dark. You stay put your back to the wall. Listening – you wait. No one… You listen to this cool darkness and – no one. In the steppe… Slowly like teeth growing you learn caution. From your milk teeth age you learn caution. Because caution – it's the milk of the steppe. It's in your skin the steppe. It bleaches your hair. It gets into your nostrils. You inhale the steppe and you exhale… You exhale its quiet fury.

Carnage. Its seed lies dormant in the boredom of winter. The grass of carnage sleeps under the snow. Boredom… In every form and shape – boredom. Boredom on the left boredom on the right, at the bottom and… boredom of the week. Boredom on Sunday when we pull the shutters early. When we don't even open the shutters. When mist goes up your sleeves. Fills everything. When suddenly the dogs fall silent. Boredom in the saucepan. Soup of boredom bread of boredom bread soft from boredom. Bread that a car brings us.

Honk Honk! We are rushing out... The old maid with frozen hands gives us a loaf. Get a move on! The oldies are running running followed by their mutts... Melancholy mutts, faithful companions in boredom. And then the last honk honk...

And then the walk back. The dead bread – is the only entertainment. The walk back... The dogs are running ahead now followed by the oldies turned into mothers... Like playful kids they look back searching their mothers' eyes.

Fleas of boredom... They explode between the teeth of the old mutts... Boredom a pool of blood. And one day yes one day it will come that day when I will tie my old neckerchief and. I will go out to fetch the bread. Honk Honk! I will hurry up running stumbling followed by my dog. Honk Honk I can hear it from here. Honk Honk... The old maid with frozen hands will hand me over the bread.

The mountains. The ocean. Like everything that is big – it is dangerous the steppe. It crushes you. You get lost. It is cruel the steppe. It leaves you to yourself. And man is a danger to himself.

Faces thousands of faces of the Great Steppe. All those tribes... It was swarming... Over the centuries in every direction. It was killing, cooking up, running riding. All those nomads. The Great Steppe is nothing but a cooking pot – it's boiling it's overflowing... And cities? All those cities? The biggest? All those St-Petersburgs, Moscows… They are nothing but valves of the Great Steppe.

Flat mugs with slanted eyes. Kalmyks, Kirghizs, Tatars, Kazakhs, Chuvashs, Bashkirs… And – here comes Pugachev. He says he's the Tsar! The true one. Peter III. The husband of Cath. Yes – of Catherine the Great. He – a Cossack, a veteran of two wars. He was saying – it's me! You, Tsarina – shame on you! Sending me down to hell… But I am here – get me if you can! You – only good to polish my shoes. The shoes of a fucking Cossack! Fucking Virgin you! I will wipe you out of the sad face of Russia. Die! You and I… I'll tie you to my saddle, bitch!

He put together an army. He only has to whistle! You can hear it from far away in the steppe. And – it comes to him. The whole steppe. All of it. In all its splendour! Fugitive serfs, Kirghizs with lacerated nostrils, tongue-less convicts, Gipsies, exiled Cossacks, soldiers of all sorts, deserters, one-eyed privates, half-wasted nobles, women three times widowed… All the scum of the steppe from before the Ural Mountains and from beyond – at his feet. Four battles won and not in the woods, no – on bare ground. In the steppe. Cities taken – big cities. Samara, Orenburg, Ufa… And the army is swelling. Every battle – Pugachev rolls in the steppe. He makes a huge ball… A miracle. The Tsarina… She looks pensive… She whistles for Suvorov. Yes – the old vigorous fox. They plot. Pugachev's comrades crack up. Betrayed, he is alone. Alone, naked, with his sword he swims across the Ural River. Big… And his army will go through hell. More cut-off ears. Hundreds more. More lacerated nostrils. Thousands more. More tongue-less screams. Trenches full of ripped-out tongues.

He will be trapped Pugachev. In the steppe – trapped. When one is betrayed – it is small the Great Steppe… Brought in a cage before Catherine he will be silent. It will be long… They will cut off his ears. Then his arms. Then – the legs. Witnesses said they hadn't taken their eyes off each other. She didn't take her eyes off his until his lights went off. He will die silent, the Cossack.

I see him my father. I see him from a distance. Spreading fishing nets – everywhere. The flat is a cobweb. I see him from here, from my little room. From this box. No bigger than a coffin. You can barely stretch – it's a comfortable wooden suit. My aunt and him. Two old spiders they are moving slowly. Saving their energy… Slow.
They don't talk. A brother and a sister they talk only at the beginning at the very beginning of the road and then – they live like fish. They see each other without acknowledging.
Among fishing nets they move. In slow motion they swim, their souls…
My father… She… They feel old. Old souls, so old they don't get caught in those nets. Souls to reap… I look at them I see them but I can't say anything. I don't know… Something nice… I'm going to sit down there in that cobweb – right in the middle… Nothing to say… Listen. Smile… Smoke and smile… See them. Let my eyes see everything. Everything.

When the goddesses arrive – the man dies. All goes and – the man dies before their eyes… From far away. The man is theirs. Their prey. When the goddesses come. When they get into his throat.

Helping my father. He is afraid of dying. He is afraid. Leaving. Alone on that trip – it scares him. Helping him to get ready. Can you do it, Dim?
He… He is going to die alone. Alone he will be in his row-boat. He knows it. No crying no weeping, no. Something soft. A chant… Yes. A soft chant.
It will be just the two of us, the two of us as often. Do you remember? As always the women are gone. Those still alive will go… All are gone. The living and the dead. Neither your mother nor your wife will be there. Everything will clear off. Everything. We'll be alone. What a weather father! A beautiful day… It snows father it snows. It's so quiet… No dogs or cats outdoors. Not even blackbirds… Not even them to blacken this whiteness.
The snow salting your wife's grave. Quietly salting the hills… The ground isn't frozen no. Not yet. You see… Everything is losing its name… Soon everything will be lost in the snow. Your friends… You. I… Our true faces… You will see neither names nor birth dates.
Death, father… Such sorrow… Your son will not have the money to bury you…

They whisper your pals… They mutter "It's not right you see… Not right at all. Your son. We know him well. But why? Eh? Why… What's going on? In France, he is… Writing, he is. Books! And his father! Dies alone! Ain't right at all."

They will whisper! I can hear them from here. Even their fingers holding a fag – I see them. You look at the yard. I will make a point of coming, in spirit I shall come. From far away. To see you… I'm coming. Ten fingers on the map – I've come. I'm here. At the door. Here…

You look far ahead. You look in my direction. To where I am. You asked me once remember – where I live? The North… The South… I took your hand – I pointed your index finger to the West.

---Read something for me---you know well. Well. I find that bit from Isaiah where he announces the slaughter in the city. Then… He wants more. That bit from Job is his favourite – "I… Behold for me nothing but the ditch the slip-knot and the grave".

His handwriting… He doesn't write anymore. His hand shakes. No more greeting cards. Not for Christmas not for birthdays. Only signatures. Bills for water heating light. An old man he is. Old. One day he won't touch a pen anymore. Not even for the accounts, not even for phone numbers… It's my aunt. He would only find her glasses for her. She takes on the job. One day he will go oral. Entirely. But that isn't the last stop… Going silent one day that – yes, that will be the last. A few years of oral only and one day – silence. Even if it's me who writes he wouldn't respond. Not in his own hand… My aunt… He would tell her write that all is well in the beehive. According to each one's age… Tell him we are happy with his letter. And to come back to the hive. To fucking come back! No not that… Don't write anything then. Don't put that in… Tell him we are not worried about him. The two of us. Not worried. And also tell him that we aren't about to start pushing up daisies… not yet… Tell him we love him. Tell him that… yes. I see them… Two spirits. Two shadows. I see him with his cigarette. Looking far away. What I have left from him… Neither his dead body nor his words. Some clothes. The smell of tobacco and his fishing nets.

What I remember of him is our sagging couch. Springs sticking out. A fat rotten walrus – ribs out.

The rug… The floor. Everything covered in hair. Everything. Old cats' hair. Mukha… Koshka. Old female cats, I see them going round and round in circles. Around him sitting… The house and the shadows… Everything will be grey from hair. I don't want to think of what I'll have left from him. Of what will get into me at the moment of his death. From him to me.

Pawning the wife's jewellery to bury her husband. Selling my mother's jewellery for the earth to take my father… Greasing Death's hand. May your sleep be peaceful. The trick. There are plenty of them memories – wholesale. It's worth having them if you haven't paid too dearly. Otherwise – nothing to resell. You must pay for your fancies. The prodigal son is back. When his mother and his father are dead. The prodigal son comes home. Hurray! Shhh! Not so loud! Myths don't work anymore. It has never worked.

Putting my father's wedding band into his mouth. For the earth to be welcoming. Putting a man into the earth. An old fish in the river. He'll be back into the stream again.

Coins to close his eyes. No. I have no coins. How would he pay the ferryman? But my father… That old fish. A fish doesn't need a ferryman to cross a river in the dark.

Let him die peacefully. I pray. During his afternoon nap. I pray. But who would reveal his death to him… Who would whisper very softly very quietly – that he's dead. So that he wouldn't be scared. So that he would know.

The cats they are going round in circles. Yawning… Mukha grey Koshka white. I see them circling. And him, a man who sleeps. His body stretched out… To us he is going to leave his body. To the white Koshka to the grey Mukha and to me.

I have no money to bury him. To pay the gravediggers and all… A mechanical digger costs too much. So – I have to dig his grave myself. Myself. No pals. I will do it. I will have to sing. A singing man is never alone. The grave has to be deep. Who knows how deep… I have to sing. I will do it. I would go down as I am digging. The sound of my spade and softly – I'm humming. Lower. Deep… Roots… Lower yet. I am going to disappear little by little. Humming soil will be all that's left. It's falling on top of me the soil… I won't hum anymore. I won't sing. I will dig in silence.

The cats will laze around, they can't help me. They will prowl about in the grass… The tall grass of the steppe… Prowl… Warm up your shadows… Sparrows and all. All the scents of the steppe… Prowl oldies prowl. It's been ages since you were let out. It will do you good.
And when I come out of his grave – I will be a thousand years old. I will be there and I will be someone else. Older than him, my dead father, older than that grass, those stones, older than the sea that had retreated from there… I will be there with the steppe. Nothing comes. Nothing happens. The horizon. Just that to extirpate your soul.

It will be over when I arrive. Lying in the middle of the street… He peed himself. It's running there. Along his leg. He fell. His head to the West towards the sunset. Our family die in the street. We die while moving, we die

outdoors, like animals who feel their end coming, we come out and then we collapse and we don't move anymore.
It works for the women like for the men. The whole family. Grandfather then my mother then him – the father. There is no one but me left. My son? No… Him – no. He is a different chapter, so he is. He swims in a different river.

Let's go… To my father lying in the street. His beard keeps growing. His hair… Blood. A small dense pool yes very dense almost black. No smell.

His hair… Can we reconstruct his soul?

The earth… Its scent was strong it smelt of spring. It disgusted me that smell. I sat down by the dead body to avoid that scent. The earth in spring and him. In our urbanless suburb my father. He was the last death of that winter.
---Is it your father? Is it really him? Answer! Do you recognise him? Why aren't you answering? You… Is it him? Is it your dad?
It was him. And – I did not recognise him at all. That stretched out man. That dense pool… And. The head yes it was his head. Smashed… like flattened a bit. Hair tarred with black blood.
His head on a pillow of blood. My father looking asleep. He loved napping and there… I see him stretched out on the tarmac. Stretched and his face… That peace… Even in the middle of his longest nap his heaviest nap he never had that face…
I couldn't take my eyes off it. The sun will go down slowly.

The return of the prodigal son. Sheep don't be scared. No one to recognise me. My aunt in the crapper, as usual. It's her headquarters. She's been constipated for centuries. She's giving up… I can hear her. Feverishly she wipes herself. She'll be running around like a lunatic. Her teeth… Lost. Dentures. Lost! It's up to me – to find them. She'll want to kiss me. We'll kiss. We'll hug… For a minute. With dignity like the Romans. Without salty liquids.

I came in and he – didn't turn around, sitting, his eyes to the West. He was still waiting for me. I've come back, I was there. Standing before him – but he kept on waiting for me. We have eaten – and he was waiting. We had tea and he was waiting. We had a smoke and he was waiting. He said to me Dim! It's you… And he was waiting for me. Waiting.

Pictures on the walls. Of those who are dead. Pictures of those who are not yet born. We are going to sell our flat. The walls are getting ready… Eyes to come… My father one day will find himself dead at the night window of this small town. Who knows… Maybe he will see it as a big one… Yes. A big city sparkling with a thousand lights…

He doesn't look at the steppe anymore… No more cigarettes. No more calendars. No more sustenance. Eyes to the West. To where I came from. To – where I will return. I see him like this for years… In the same position. Years will go by, I see him there, his eyes to the West. I will grow old and he will be there. His hands his hair his old age… He is there for centuries. The man won't grow older anymore. No breathing. Everything will stop. Days moons seasons… Timeless. Motionless. An empty shell of a man. I will come back again and again. I always leave things behind. My clothes, my laptop. But I will never see him like before.

Brother-Sister… They will tear each other apart. One day. Twilight… So long to cross. Twilight coming… The yard, that summer yard becomes huge. Empty…

The block of flats dies. Small noises die down. Unbearable and quiet their past life comes closer comes into the yard.

They can't find their place. Turning round and round in circles but it's alright, it's still alright. Now they insult each other. And I hide everything that is sharp. For the moment… But if I forget, if I leave if I leave a knife on the table… They squabble half-heartedly. Without warmth. Brother-Sister. He took her scarf. But his jumper! She snatched his jumper! My glasses! I can't find them… Where… Where… And here they are! She had been wearing them for three days…

---But it's disgusting! ---You piss everywhere! ---Even on the walls! ---Do you want me to hold it? Do you want me to hold it straight for you? ---Sit down to piss for fuck's sake! ---Sit down! ---Time for you to sit down---
One day he will kill her. He will kill her and pee on her dead body. Standing. He will tell the cops "Ten years that old bag wanted me to pee sitting". It will make them laugh, father.
Their smell and everything… they are alike – more and more. Like potatoes. They like the same things at the same time. I imagine sometimes that they kill each other… So close to each other. One day I tell myself they won't be able to tear each other apart. They will grab yes… Knifes to cut them off each other – and they will kill themselves. At last… They will get there.

I'm alone and it's night. I write these pages in the Russian night. My old father is sleeping, my aunt too, they have become two talking crutches. If one falls, the other does too. They talk… Talk… It's the day's music. Dogs – it's the night. It's the night's music.

They are scared of the end. Brother-Sister. Fear has bent them. Death… Two trees that make an arch. But they are sleeping now, so quiet.

I hear stray dogs. They bark out the darkness, they howl their song in the distance. It comes and goes that music, it keeps me company night after night. Their chant soars. Water that floods the Volga's islands – this chant rises towards me. To my room, up to my eyes. That night chant… Every night. It flows from my fingers. It soils the pages. They become black my pages. Black. Nothing can happen to me anymore… Nothing more. When the pages turn black… It's so light.

I say – Alex… The steppe is so slow my friend. Everything is slow here. Life is teaspoon-fed, but it's a bit itchy and – it's an abyss. I will bring you some bread Alex. Some bread from here. Dark… Heavy. If I survive.

I have a friend here, a puppy, he was lost, he follows me, he's become my son. I am a dog Alex, so I am. He's always with me. Everywhere. He eats on the landing. He doesn't want to come into the flat, he looks straight into my eyes, straight in the eyes he looks and goes away. He knows I'm going to betray him he feels it. I know what will happen when I'm no longer here. You have to find your pack son.

To be close to the window. So close to the night. The night of a small town… A night without promises… To get slowly closer to the darkness. The glass… To be so close to the darkness. Your eyes search rummage run in the dark and. There is nothing. Nothing… Your eyes… They come back empty-handed. Your eyes, these hunting dogs run into the night and hunt shadows then come back. No quarry.
To be so close to the night. Your reflection… The night is looking at you. I… Who am I?

I say – rage. The quiet rage of the night – comes out of me. Comes out… Night comes out of me, out of my skin. Go... Go back home. You can't look away… My eyes, come back to me. Come back wolf cubs. My eyes… Have seen so much… Have forgotten so much… Don't be afraid. My eyes… Come back. Forget the night. Forget what you have seen… Yes. This night and. I in front of it. I am the face of the night. Who am I? Who…

Here everything is more real than anything I've written. The soil here is mud… Tyre tracks in the steppe. The heat here. I must write with soil with mud. I must use it. Here… On a page in my diary – I've written mud mud mud.

Packed with clay – the steppe. Bloody brown. It rains one day it rains two days it rains three. Mist… It rains at night. It rains at dawn. It rains it rains to go hang yourself.

The steppe is smooth. The boots carry five kilos of mud. We all become dwarfs with feet of clay.

It rains and then it stops dead. For half an hour – the rains forget to rain. The heat… The heat, the cicadas that drive you mad. And then the sun and the steppe cracks at last. First – fissures and then it splits open. It's exhilarating the steppe at noon. It rips its own skin like a mad woman, a mad woman at midday. The sun breaks it. Its clay skin. If you lie down if you look at it like this – you see those big clay scales. Waves waves as far as you can see.

It's become so difficult… To touch the earth. To really touch it. It used to be so close the earth… Dry. It is so close the earth. Hot… Hot. An oven. The air is dancing to make you fall. Dancing… Bones blades of grass. Broken cricket shells. Dried up insects. Thousands thousands of carcasses, of small bones. Of big ones. Thousands of screams, of calls in the silence of the earth. Under the nails of the earth. Before me. Hot… Grey. I looked at it as if it were the sea. I plunged my hands into the burning earth. As if to wash them. It's so hot. Such silence the earth and such peace.

Markets never change. Like the flies come back to a rotting carcass people come back to sell stuff at the same place. Nothing has changed here. Thirty years…

I loathe markets. All markets.

I am looking for fish for my aunt. She'll eat it by herself. Bones – to the cats… She would like a big one… That's why I'm loitering here. I can't slip away quickly. I've seen them already… Thirty years? So fresh… These fish I had seen them with my father.

As a kid I always waited for him to come back from fishing. I used to hide in his bed… He would come in. Noiselessly like a cat yes a cat coming back from hunting. Heavy with the night… He would undress in the dark. Heavily he would lie down… He smelt of the river. Big waters… He would fall asleep in the blink of an eye. A big stone thrown into the water.

His sleep and then – he would disembowel the fish. Often pike and inside – sometimes there was a little one. A small faded green perch. Its quarry of the night perhaps.

He always gave me those small fish. He would push it with his big finger… Towards me. He would push towards me that little piece of tissue on a slippery board. And would continue to deal with the big one. Tenderly.

Always the same. Disembowelled fish… Fish on the market… Old women's fingers in the wounds… They move their fingers and – that sound like when you separate pinched lips. Pearly wounds of the fish. The pale wounds...

The old women get money for the innards. They choose slowly, hands plunged into the basins full of, yes you would say full of snakes... Those innards. The blind old fingers. The old women get up early. After midnight. They roam roam those morning choughs... Fat, pregnant with dawn. With today. It's long, that morning when the old women wake up at midnight and – go to the market. All night they walk walk... It's long that dawn when the lorries burst open and the smell of blood cold smell jumps into the nostrils. The drivers get off, open their fridges.

It happens to me at the markets... Visions... Hands with no name or face. Bunches of black grapes. Women's fingers plunged into the heart of a bunch of grapes... Blue in rapture. Blue that collapses into black. A severed head of a bull... The severed head of Dionysus. On a tray... His hair... His washed curls... Closed eyes of women when they plunge into the heart of a bunch of grapes... Their hands... In a dream. Those hands – their name is nobody.

Life is so sad fundamentally. So naked in the eye of the dead. So clear... Family is hell. They are all horrible. Yes. All. Hidden love and cordial hatred here's their basic sustenance. Who fucks who – no matter, the mother fucked by the son who is fucked by his father who in turn had been deflowered by some Goliath at the dawn of time. And that moves sways vibrates guzzles lives. It's too serious all that too heavy. But for the dead it's a laugh yes, hilarious. For those who are on the other side it becomes so remote. To laugh at this all... You have to die first. To croak. Yes Dim – pay at the checkout.

Boredom… Cosmic boredom. My aunt… She's bored to death. Day after day she dies of boredom but can't manage to croak. She pretends to die just like she has been pretending to live all her life.
I thought about all this cheerfully. Disconnected for a while. I shouldn't have. She talks about interesting things. She tells me about the dead. Neighbours… Do you remember such and such? She tells me everything. Their agonies hours stages. Everything. How and where… All the details. She looks younger! Alright – I say. Let her stack it up… All the sorrows of the world. All the cancers. All the tumours… Arteritis, arthrosis, colitis, cystitis and varicose veins… Everything. Psoriasis, eczema… From the smallest things to the biggest. To the end – yes, to the very end of pain. All the dead women of the neighbourhood in my ears – let them rush in. Even those who didn't know they had lived. All! I open my ears for them. My aunt poor girl. Let her spill it. Let her vomit this life, poor woman! From the bottom of her soul. To scrape the bottom… Let all that sadness stream. Let it flood me. The vomit of life is flooding me. The vomit, the old life of centuries of vomit. Let it rise as vomit. We shall float light as chicken shit. I, she, my father and the cats and this room and all. I'll immerse myself into it like a silent oyster… A wise oyster. So speak to me aunt. Pounce! Go to the bottom of it. Tell me my mother, her death and all. I'm all yours, let's talk – you and I.
After the death of my father my aunt will sell the flat to pay for a room in an old women's home. Before leaving she'll put the two cats down. Mukha the grey and Koshka the white. She will dig a small grave in the forest, put them in together. Those two that hated each other when they were alive will stay there, stretched out, back to back, peaceful.

And then she will go, half-mute, arrogant, to live among other old women and will die quietly, one morning, at dawn, of heart failure.

I am not looking for her presence here. My mother. For signs... Her spirit isn't here anymore. Her spirit has left this house. There are photos – yes but she isn't here anymore. My aunt... They didn't get along at all and now she wins. The ground is all hers. The photos too. My mother hated her picture being taken and now... There are pictures of her everywhere – to chase away her spirit. All memories have their pornographic side.

Father... To keep it all under control... I was sure of myself. To keep it all under control! My delirium... That I could tame him. To wake up the demons and then – tame them. To make them come... Make them crawl make them slave for me...

Not possible oh no it is not possible. No one can do anything. Anything. I can do nothing. Not I not anyone. Not even a movement. One can control nothing. Not the big finger not the index not a pupil. When it hurts one screams. Full stop. We can't control anything, father... Not you not I not anyone. We are scared and we can do nothing. The army. Then mama. My son. Writing... Sleeplessness. My dead. I have opened the lid! Just a bit! They have all come out... My demons! I've barely moved the pot and there you go – screwed.

I had too much cooking, father. All the families, yes, all – we have too many pots on the fire and one day it explodes. I – I couldn't keep it under control anymore, the fire. How could I cover all those pots? With only one lid?

Mate! But that's what it was – a scullery boy in a witch's kitchen, that was the thing, father. We can't keep the lid on anything. Chasing the demons... Chasing them down to your feet... Keeping them under your soles. Yes but we don't keep anything under control. Peeing around to keep the demons away? Making a magic circle of piss?...

It flows it trickles it blows up it cracks it explodes it smokes it spurts from all parts and there is nothing we can do... I could neither bring down the fire nor cover the cooking pots. That's the true issue father. And mama... And then – him, her lover. Your best friend. He was your pal. Pal... But what did... he die of? Dead. Mama too. All is gone all... And us, father? You and I. Does it make any sense... Scratching the bottom of old pots? Maybe we'll live a lot longer you and I.

I see you going far away. Fishing with your pals and then alone. You take out your nets. In the mist, yes, I see your nets in the fog... Your shape. You bend over to take out the fish. Dull like old coins. And you – you pick them... Slowly. You move... In a dream... Your hands feel... rampage in the water... Seek the extremity of the net and. You pull it all out in one go. I see swags swags of sleeping fish. They don't move anymore. You, slowly you entangle them a tired fisherman. You only fish at night. In a dream, you catch sleeping souls. But yours... It isn't with you. Yours is in town! With them. Your pal and your wife. Them... You stop for a moment... With a fish in your hand. You look at it. You would like to sew up every mouth, yes, of every fish – to stop them telling you about those two... Your wife and her lover. Sew up the mouths of all the fish in the Volga... For them to keep the secret. For you to stop knowing. To stop thinking. To never think again. At all. At all.

I can't wait to go. I say – even mountains lose patience. Patience. But I can't wait can't wait… Everything here tells me – be slow. You have to be slow… Slow. Like this earth and the stray dogs and the mud, slow like these young poplar trees nodding in the wind. Slowly…
Slow like the sunsets in these lands. Slow like the snow that will cover those remote forests. Slow like the glacial nights when we were alone you and I – Babania in her house lost in the white sheets of snow – and around us shadows were gliding gliding… There were howls and I said very quietly – WOLF.
Slow like a seed in the soil that is searching its way out. Slow like old people taking little sips of life. Slow… Slow…

I had to go father. I am drifting. I took the bus. To leave! Far from this steppe. To leave! To never come back! From here I was looking far away, so far that I could see the land of Genghis Khan. There he lived as a kid. There, they were hunting marmots, he and his brothers, and then when his father was poisoned they were reduced to poverty. As a friend, he had a bird, a falcon. An old falcon, yes, he was so old that he couldn't hunt and Temujin hunted for him.

The Great Steppe! To never go back to these lands. I say – no. Never again.
Far from here. To go to Damiana… To the woman. She is real the woman, not the steppe… No. To a woman. To the Volga. To the edge of Asia. The left bank – the steppe, Asia. The right bank, the red mountain – Europe. To leave. To turn my back to it endlessly – I'm running for my life…

Genghis Khan and all… All these bloody clouds… The march of his army… The steppe is lynx-eyed but the lynx is sleeping. Come on! Salvation doesn't come from here anymore. My father, yes, him – he was dreaming of Genghis Khan. Of the Mongols… He talked and talked to me about it. My whole childhood he talked talked… He got drunk on it once and for all. The Great Steppe at the time of the sword. He knew lots! The steppe, the great Temujin, Batu Khan, his grandson, every single thing. Like one of his Noyons. But enough now – fed up with it all. With that endless lowland that swallows your soul. With that dry sea that slits your eyes. Now – enough. Never again – those mugs of the steppe. Those large faces, those cheekbones. All sorts of cheekbones. Hordes waves flat faces. Passing through… Swallowed, all. First him, Genghis Khan and then all the others. His children. His grandson. Batu Khan, that wise man with a sword. I could barely walk – and already… Those stories… My father's dreamy eyes. Every spring Temujin awakens. He roams around, a saturnine spirit. He calls his army. He looks for his heart buried somewhere in the Great Steppe… The legend says – he will be back one day. In all his glory. He will find his heart's tomb. He will unearth it and Asia will awaken for the second time. Frightened earth will close its eyes…
The Mongols… In the Great Steppe tumens and tumens. An ocean of horsemen. Clouds of them! Seven days a week not leaving the saddle – a childhood habit. And their crossing of the mountains? The Tian Shan. A year! Crawling secretly, noiselessly and – anything with a tongue – slashed. One year – to crash down on the sultan like a storm. Mahomet-the-all-powerful! He didn't expect them there, from that side! He was preparing for a teaspoons battle,

the wimp! For ten days was he waiting seething at the walls of Bukhara. Girls' fight at the dinner table! And when he turned round his Arabian stallion… He saw the sea rolling straight over the city. And then… he saw the sun going down in fear. He saw the sky crawling. They were deploying slowly… Tumens… Clouds of Mongols. And it was all over for the city. But for that – a year in the snows of Tian Shan. Without waking up ounces, those snow leopards that sleep wrapping their tails around like scarves. They were climbing… Climbing. Food – they baked their bread under camel's legpits. Where did they learn that? From other tribes? Long gone since… Their headless shadows wandering in the Great Steppe…

Mongol cavalry – horses that didn't know stables or oats. Anything under their hoofs, that – yes. A Mongol – living in the saddle. Sleeping in the saddle. Riding all day riding all night. Riding in his dream, riding in his sleep, trotting in his waking dream. Without talking without washing. Hair – it grows three times faster during the war. You should have seen them… You should have been there! When they were flooding the plains of Central Asia… Mahomet saw wild gods riding bears. And their cries! Those cries… Ya ha! Ya ha! They swept everything all the way to Hungary. Europe, that lacy soul hearing those battle cries it didn't know where to shit! What could it do against those Ya ha!... The Mongol shattered the proud knees of the West. He saw the Danube River. He watered his horses. And there – he stopped. Oh all that, father… you gave me the Mongol disease. They always frightened me your wild rides.

But now – I leave. I missed the first bus – otherwise I would have been gone at dawn. But what a stir in the balls!

They're freaking out down there... You have balls the size of chickpeas Dim!

But what? Comrades of the lost army – that's what... The revenants will come back. They are looking for you... I receive letters, signs. My father has witnessed it. They write on the mailbox – Die! With ketchup yes, for the moment, but blood – it will come. It isn't the Yakuts, no. Or just one... Zachary. I won't forget you, no. You – neither, you won't forget me.

Revenge Yakut style! They are more efficient than the angels. When God is weighing your skin – they are already on their way. In the cities they feel lost. Always in groups talking to no one. They stick together in threes, fours and speak only in Yakut. Once wronged they bite like snakes. Delayed revenge. From then on your life is just a rubber band. Not worth more than a wormy apple... You have already forgotten them... Those three arseholes with Mongol mugs... They all look alike like potatoes but they – they don't forget. They hunt you. They track you down day and night. You can laugh cry phone your lawyer the police run around like mad find bodyguards bulletproof vests! Or forget. You can look through the window, fuck all the women you can find, sing in the loo, sign contracts, even get sick... Anything. They will find you and bump you off. Without pity or anger. They don't open your dead eyes to spit into them. No. Without any anger they will take you down from a distance and leave. They kill a fox in the eye from thirty metres. To have its fur intact... I know what I'm talking about. I saw them at work. They don't sow bullets, no. They plant them.
Before they go hunting – I saw that – they gather stones. They sing around them and then plant their knives into it... Into the pile of stones. It's you...

You are the prey. You can turn into stone, into a mosquito, into a snake, into a fly – they will find you and they will kill you.
Walking in the night-time streets… Their squinting eyes like asleep… They don't whisper into your ear no. They smash it squarely.
Their patience… And even if you know how to read the signs, the omens, that twilight book of the small cities in the Great North – you are already a dead body. A dead body that Death just let out to pee. They will come and they will plant a bullet in your eye. With their 7.62. Hunting rifle, Kalashnikov model. Patience… They will wait for you everywhere. Near your home. At work. At your girlfriend's… Even in the snow… Day and night they will live in tents in the middle of the city and they will get you.

And all that… All that – for a small swindle. So banal for us… A tiny little everyday diddle… For a tiny little swizzle! They blow up your head. And the diamonds… For those gems and the price he paid for them… Zachary. I can write my will. No draft. No need to bother.

They are ghosts… But it will be for real. Fucking real my bloodbath. Real… Not to imagine. To pass out. You will want to lick the ground. To crawl. To eat your snot. To croak and not only once. To croak for real. Full stop.

Why have you unearthed them? They must be left to sleep in the soil of the Great North. Sleep. Caught in the ice. For eternity.

They will come. The revenants. Vengeful… They will find bodies to inhabit. Whatever. There are bodies lying around… Here in this godforsaken land. I know it and that's why I run. Faster than a bitch that smells a dead body coming. I know the signs. I can read them. Yesterday a hawk cried yes, cried above my head! In the middle of the town! So many people around… I recognised that cry. It came from the other side of life… I recognised it. It's far-seeing a hawk, yes, far and I know the steppe. The steppe is pregnant with everything.

I get off at the bus station. Samara… The storm throws the dust up. Towers of dust! I can't see my hand. Wind from the desert. Wind from the arch-South. The demons blow hot! From the Gobi from the Sahara from all those crazy places, those mad saunas. The oven of the desert is open.

I can feel a thunderstorm coming. In a couple of minutes the first spits will shrivel in the dust fine like brown flour.

Another bus… It goes down to the Volga. Then – I run under the drops big like marbles. Like a scared fox I almost fly. Hop! I run avoiding pools escaping drops. I fly to the hotel. Phew! Three more pools to jump over and – I'll be there. I'll crash down there. At last… No more steppe! Never again. Only Damiana. Only that girl and her shadow by the bed. Damiana… In the flesh and in the blood and her shadow there. The flowers on the wallpaper. And the thunderstorm… Lights go off. Crack-brommbrrromm… It's rolling from afar. And then – it rumbles! It booms! I feel the walls trembling. Crack-brommm! This hotel, this damn lousy hut – is going to cave in any second! The cannons of the Great Steppe are rumbling.

II

And then – the awkward stuff. The money issue. Money. Talk about a needle in a haystack! I write to Clara. Some money! From Samara – Victor tied to my back – I write. Some money. My SOS sent once – I copy and paste. Only the first names change – I send my arrows. To every corner of France. Some money. To Clara in Rochefort. To Gouk and his ladylove in Paris. To the South, even to women I barely know. To old ones to young ones. To book club members. At your feet! I say to them – I'm at your feet. Not only women, I write to men too – some money. A whore, so I am, son. Money, just a little… I don't even have a heel of a loaf to spread my caviar on, friends. All I do is write. Twelve hours a day. I'm a paperfucker. Twelve hours. Fucking hell! I am writing and I am dying, girls. I have one pair of socks left. The fans are grabbing everything. Am I kidding? Come on… A little bit of dough into my gloved hands. Or else I kick the bucket. A little bit of money – if only to bury me. And they reply reply the girls. By letter. They laugh. Especially Clara, oh she's having her fun. "Come on poor Raspu-dim… Put on your lacy skirt, princess! My poor baby… Dim-the romper… Big deal – you just have to pee sitting. You will have to muddle through by yourself. Like us. Get married!"

They laugh, the girls… "I'm going to get myself a cat! A big tomcat! A real one… I'll call him Dim and get him neutered!"… The ones who don't laugh – are spiteful. Gouk – write when your balls are empty! Like a Saint! It's easier to decipher a cow's mooing than your ramblings. Mysticism for a repentant whore. Reaching out to the stars from his gutter, the little shit… Natasha, yes, it's her, her. I see her dictating his letters.

The true friends of the artists – it's the old women. The oldies never betray. It's the artists who betray them.

Am I laughing? Maybe… One night a very dark one and – I am on the other side. My rowboat is full. And it's been a while, friends.

Trying to climb out of the sewer, am I? My shoes are leaking. Like my mother I wrap plastic bags around my feet first – and then shoes. It helps a bit. Clara wrote – she wants to buy me English shoes. Yes the posh ones. The everlasting ones. They will put me in the coffin with them on. The thought of it…

I shoot to the four corners. SOS missiles. To the Moldovans too, yes, to Theodore. He loved my *Fritz*. He made them all read it, yes, his whole gang of literate gypsies. In Bucharest, too. I am throwing it – he said – over the Carpathians.

There… in the blue woods three girls are dreaming of it! The three vampiresses! Licking their lips. I saw them… Three photos. Vampiresses, trues ones. He's not kidding Theo, they want to host me. So that I could scribble on and on… They are all in for board and lodging. For my tranquillity, my arse. Those three girls… Plum brunettes. Arch-bachelorettes, ha! More gothic than Hell. They want to meet Dim – says my Theo. They have a bear! An old one... He's nice... He's diabetic. You just have to nod – they will come and pick you up at your father's...

Alright. It makes me dream, right... Let's give it a try – let them send me some money. A little bundle of love... For my fare all the way to the castle. I am coming. Don't be mean, girls. So little dough... Don't wake the Count, no need... I am coming. After. First – the bundle, then – I. Otherwise – we can still have fun but in a different way. A nice little bundle for my blood. 200 ml for 200 euros. One glass... One glass of my vermillion. No kidding. A glass of blood, mine, freshly drawn. From this morning, girls.

It didn't work at all. Apart from writing – calling. I had to cry and moan and whisper – some money... I was using all kind of phones. All sorts of phone cards. I was even calling from the army barracks. From indoors and from outdoors. Strolling. Waltz music playing... Giving rhythm to soldiers' step... On the banks of the Volga people are waltzing... "The Blue Danube", "The Hills of Manchuria"... "All Dead in Mukden"...

There were so many caps around – you would think it was war. Squaddies of every variety strolling arm in arm on the quays. Quays ending – trotting in the sand. Couples, threesomes, groups. Tepid evenings – beer, beer, beer. And then – legs spread pissing from the quay farther afield. Into the waters of the Volga. Boots wet – come on... farther still. The loser pays the next round.

So I asked them nicely – offering some booze – to use their radio. What?! Where? In France? Fucking hell! Go ahead! Is it true? Your chick! Say hi to her from us! How do they fuck the chicks there? Under the armpits?

That's how I called you all, girls. From the steppe, from my headquarters. I was saying to them – I'm calling you from the place where Tamerlane fought Tokhtamysh! It was here, exactly. Precisely. I'm on the top of a hill. Under my feet – thousands of dead warriors… I shouted! The connection was dropping all the time… Can you hear me? And like this? No? It's Dim… Whew… I'm calling you from the banks of the Volga.

Hands up with the radio… Waves licking my arse… I called you all. My girls… My dear life-rings. You fancied that big time, there… In France. With your concierge sentimentality. They nearly cried. It isn't every day that I call you from an army radio… From some 3000 km and a bit. Dream! Eleven fingers on the map… Radio, distant sounds of commands… And not in French. In Russian… Wow! It gives you goose-bumps. Brrr! The Red Army in motion. Oh that Slavic soul… I put you to work. Let it tackle it. I warmed you up, girls… I made you laugh – love – cry – sniff – and laugh… It makes you lose weight all that. And you… I would make the sun set at noon – for you. Four hours ahead. I was making myself grow old faster… But that didn't work either. Alright – I say, girls. Alright. All is in flames, as Buddha used to say. I say – all is in smoke. Men women hearts words – all burns out quickly. And all is left is smoke. That's what makes your eyes sting, girls.

I called Clara. Her voice… So close… Clara… You ask me how are things and then you cry. Cry… I forget everything. To comfort you Clara. To make you laugh… From afar… You. Let's talk quietly… You're love Clara. Listen to the steppe. Here. Do you hear it? So calm tonight. Resting… Warm. And my mother is resting too. Buried somewhere there. I don't know… I didn't go. Not yet… It's a new graveyard… She is too. Love. And grass here is love.

A bit burnt but love. And the dogs there… They are love too. They don't know it but they are love… And you yes. You too, love. I… Not always. Yes, Clara, I'm here. Even the piece of bread in my bag is love. I'm going to eat it with ham. It's a bit too salty but it's love too. And when you are going to pee it will also be love. I'm going to do it now. For you. And you, in Paris for me. I had to tell you Clara… All of that. Yes. With a smile. Very softly. Without breathing. Clara… This has to be written on sheets of paper curling in the fire. What is happening to us is immense…

People were saying no. That forest you will never go there. Never. Not with me – they were saying… Why the hell do you want to go there? You've forgotten everything. You are coming from far away. You aren't from here anymore… Drop it… You aren't from here.

At the time pregnant girls were going there. They were going in at night. Heavy. The next day – out empty. Now – it's cats' and dogs' grounds. The oldies bury their pets there. A dream place. They call it "the nasty forest". They have always called it that, yes, but my mother… She wasn't afraid. Not of the dead, not of the ghosts. She was afraid we wouldn't make it to her payday, that yes. Since then – she died. I'm alone here. I'm putting off seeing my father. He no longer knows if I'm still here or not.

Sleeping? I don't sleep anymore. The demons have tattooed my eyelids… "don't let them sleep!" The question is – diamonds. My treasure… I brought them from Yakutia… enough to live on. How could I otherwise… ten years with no boss. No slaving away. No grinding… My war treasure. Here is the lovely thing. I had buried them well the dead guys' diamonds. It hadn't been easy. I had to find a buyer. There are some now… not many of the real ones but there are some. At the time of my military service… it was easier to find old pants you'd never farted in… than a real buyer. Oh my little gems… dragon's teeth… I sowed them all… I planted them deep… and the patience. Patience Dim… The stealth of a snake… I was waiting… at the worst times I was thinking of them. Buried three feet under. Fireflies in the earth. Precautions taken… when you plant the future – you have to plant it deep. And then I see that girl, hanging around the fire. Prowling… brushing the dragon's teeth. So near those tears of snow. So near those drops of Nordic Gods' sap… It was a hidden place. A secret place. This young woman alone… Like a sudden apparition.

It's the third time… The third night that I come here. I visit it… My war treasure. I want to see them to touch them to make sure they're here… Under the apple tree… I have to dig them up. But she's around that girl! The third time that she's here! The dice miracle… She looks like a vixen. A vixen so sure of herself… We shall see who will be digging it, girl… I'm no mug. But she doesn't go… straight into my eyes she looks… And there something happens. I see her strange face, like a mask. It lasts the blink of an eye, and then nothing… She doesn't speak to me, no but I see her lips moving… "What are you rummaging for here? Chasing a spirit?" She smiles… a long smile. I see her pointy teeth… "The name of the demon… The name of the demon – it's you".

…It's sultry. Sultry… I'm dripping… She turns her back to me. Slowly. She goes away. It's an invitation… one step, two… I see her dress with a pattern of red flowers…

moving away. Tree trunks… the will-o'-the-wisp, I still see it. Just about… It's then, exactly then that the die was cast. I don't feel my own body, as if asleep… The trap was set and I jumped into it. All is there. All is said there.

My diamonds my babies. To get you out of here… To France… There. To decide… to find a buyer… There were some but in Moscow… I lost touch. New ones? I – I'm nothing to them, a gnat… Small enough to pass in-between their teeth. Not worth a fart in a blizzard. I have only FIVE of them left. They would laugh but laugh! The buyers… Only five stones? Are you kidding… For that… And the papers? It's tough now. Times have changed… We are still open for business but… swimming in murky waters? That's over now. The FSB are not joking. I can hear them… Buyers here – forget it Dim. My stones… I have to get you out of here. But the scanners and all… I must get them out. Under my skin… The pocket in my wrist… I made it with a knife. Specially for the gems, some twenty years ago.

I'm in the red. I have diamonds in the ground and I'm in the red. It's annoying… I'm a pauper. As usual I'm seeking the fifth corner in my room! When I think about my paternal great-grandmother… Eudoxia… She had servants! She wasn't mixing with the poor… Not at all and then the Revolution! That October stirred them all together. My father, he got himself a peasant's daughter. And on that side, those peasants, they endured the Great Famine. The famous famine… On the Volga… What a life…

We haven't done well Dim. Not well at all… Always on the side of the poor. Right down in the sewer and no dough. Still no dough. I have a ten euro bill left. I'm thinking of photocopying it. Maybe notarising it, even... Before converting it... Damned be the rouble.

Gem trafficking. Diamonds. Danger and youth... It was in the North. Always the North. The damned place... I'm still a bit fidgety about it.

Zachary, Elia, Joseph, David, Daniel... it was at the beginning of time. Straight out of the Bible. The Yakuts were converted to Christianity forcibly... Names changed. Baptised. All. Even the old people. The dying included. No more "The First Snowflake" and the like... Then – alcohol... the white man planted his cross in the frozen ground. The tundra abandoned its children. There were some who didn't want that... they were keeping a low profile and living as before.

Zachary is short. He taught me how to sleep in the snow. Choose. Dig. Protect your feet with newspapers. White man's boots don't hold the warmth at all. I saw what Zachary was doing. He never complained. He would wrap his feet with newspaper sheets and that's it. Warm. It was him who taught me how to smuggle the little stones. He was fond of me. His father was a shaman. An alcoholic he was.

At the time there were no scanners. They were frisking us head to toe. In all the holes that link us to the world. In all the fresh wounds. They were searching everywhere with their fingers but not in our cells. That would have been be the last lick! So – it was him, Zachary who made my first pouch for the little stones. Their little home. You sew it up and tie the thinnest fishing line to it. Tie it good. A pouch to swallow. You tie the other end to a tooth. Then you eat a piece of white bread. A glass of milk... the pouch holds on for two days. You don't shit for two days… and then you pull it out.

We – those who worked indoors… I, Nicholas, Victor, Zachary… We would bring the stones to the shaman. To Zachary's. We would shit our treasures outdoors. Delicately… One by one. Then we would bury them. It was the shaman, Zachary's mad father who knew where the diamonds' grave was. No one else, I was sure. We trusted neither dogs nor reindeer. We were covering our arses like virgins! But when Nicholas and Victor took off – it was all over, the peace and quiet. Zachary's father changed the hiding place. For all of them. Mine and his sonny's.

But those two poor buggers… Nico and Vic… They were caught rummaging in their frozen shit. Five years of military fortress. Zachary and I – we sewed our mouths. Not a stir. Not a step. Waiting for the peace and quiet to come back steady.

But the stones had vanished! He didn't know what to think, Zachary. He couldn't contemplate suspecting his old man… I could. He became joyful, the shaman… He was all dreamy, a big smile on his face. But I didn't know WHERE. Where he hid them. Where… The whole tundra… And thirteen little stones somewhere there. It was fucked.

It was Zachary who found them. He wanted some medication. For his father… He didn't shit for two weeks his dad. We looked at each other Zachary and I. We looked at each other and we understood. The shaman hunt was launched.

Our treasure… Mine and his… we were going crazy little step by little step. I was watching out for Zachary all the time. I wouldn't take my eyes off him. My little treasure… Drops of the sperm of the North… Here we come!

He went to his old man's. He said – "to pay him a visit", my arse! When I got there – it was all over. I saw his father lying on the ground. His belly open… His guts… They were spilling out… too much guts for an old man. I didn't touch anything. Just a glance and then crept back. Flat on the ground. His gun wasn't there. Usually under his head… it was his pillow – it wasn't there anymore. On the lookout Dim.
Not even a dog. Zachary had killed them all. I crawled a bit. I had to move… Around the shack. And – there it was… Far far away a figure. Tiny tiny – crouching maybe a hundred metres away. Digging… That how it was.

No landmark. I was searching something to lock my eyes on. No stones no trees and Zachary is digging. Zachary is sowing! I close my eyes to memorise the place. It didn't work, I was losing the image.

And then – I got an idea. A stone! Dig Zachary… Claw well. And then cover it. I crawl behind the shack. Come on Dim move your arse. Find a stone… Not too big not too small. A piece of rope, a knot and – you have it. The rope… The stone tied to it… But dig Zachary dig… Hide them hide… And you my stone we have only one chance… I'm calm. I have to aim well… He won't look at the stone. He will run away Zachary. I have to aim well. I hear the purring of a car. It's getting closer… Come on… Zachary hears it too… Throw!
My stone hits him on the back. He woke up fast, but fast! Dropped everything, jumped up like a rabbit. Then the car…
I would like to become a stone. For an hour… For half an hour. To be still, with the cord around. To mark the grave of my dear drops.

They didn't look for me. They came especially for you Zachary. An officer. The five squaddies… Especially for you… Thank you, dad. You had anticipated the thing but too late. You have to thank your father, Zachary. Handcuffs and all… I thought I could see Zachary's eyes. Locked on the diamonds in the ground… He was crying… The dragon's teeth in the ground started to move… He could feel them in the ground, Zachary… He could feel them going away. He could do nothing about it.

My stone was spot on. One hour and they were mine. Here… In my fist and in my belly… Thirteen crystal tears. Hooked to three teeth – in my grip. That's how it happened.

On the beach… It was almost dark. She asked me for a light, then a cigarette. And when I said – even my lungs – she smiled. Slowly… She knew her power. I hadn't recognised her at first. I asked her how much she charged. She smiled again. That girl knew her power… She pays for her cigarette… She tells me – a kiss…

She lay down by my side on her tummy. Her gaze above my shoulder. We were in the darkness. At her second pull on the fag I recognised her. I felt… her breath. That girl… Like in a dream… When the body is a feast. A feast…

The full moon is a call. A call from someone who doesn't even exist… A being. A voice. A woman.

A woman's mane. The roots of her soul. If you touch it… If she lets you stroke it… and her eyes. She would close them. You would touch her soul.

I wasn't drunk, no. I saw her walking alone on the sand. She was singing. Crystal eyes… Smiling lips… I looked at her close up. A young drunken shadow. A drunken goddess… We took the magic train… Bewitched… I was in danger.

My life with two prostitutes… It won't be heavy. And then their son Victor. It will be light-hearted… Like a little family. Here. In the East… Far far to the East.

Victorius – Dimitrius salutes thee. That made them laugh. Laugh! The Roman salute. Fist on the heart. Then an open hand stretched out. Dimitrius to Victorius! Offering your heart on your palm. Those who are about to rock thee – salute thee! They were falling over with laughter. Those who are about to feed thee – salute thee! Hail Victorius! My milk is Yours. For You, Your Somnolence – my blood.

He's only one year old, Victor, and he's big. He's clean and he's a thinker. One night I taught him how to pee standing. Like a man. We peed together in unison, gazing into the sky. Turning our backs to the river.
Valentina was proud so so proud! Victor he peed especially for her. Standing. Like a real man. And since then she leaves the kid with me. He's gold for her, he's the day and the night. Her biggest sorrow. Her maddest joy. And I – am the kornak in this.
Damiana never brought clients to the room. Never to the hotel. Valentina – oh yes, she did. As soon as I would see a guy coming or even before – her heels' click-click and the guy's heavy steps – I would leave the room with Victor in my arms. Destination – the hotel bar.

Valentina… She laughs – you are a true father hen… I am hiring you! The careful babushka! I'm buying you tripe soup! I'm leaving Vic to you! All I do is spreading them but you – a real mummy! How do you fucking do it? He loves you… There's a trick there! Stay with us… Six more months and we'll have the wallet full to bursting. We'll go to my old mama's.

She's bouncy Valentina. She's small round and. Bouncy like a small ball.

---There're guys who like it! ---I say to them do you want me to fart to show you the entrance! ---But they are shy the guys! ---So fucking shy! ---they take their hard-on seriously! ---You ---when you get a boner ---you're never too serious ---you don't get hard at all then?! ---Come on ---Show me your limp noodle ---Take out your worm ---There's no such thing as a pointless hard-on! ---You! I love you! ---

Her eyes are laughing… Laughing.

---But beware if I didn't sleep well ---I become naaasty! ---A fairy with an axe! A foul-mooded fairy so I am ---Have you ever seen a foul-mooded fairy? ---Oh then – you haven't seen anything…

When the weather was sunny – we were going to the Volga, to the sands. He liked playing in the hot sand. When it rained – we came down to the bar.

Victorius adores television. Sitting on my lap before the screen he wouldn't move. Fascinated he would watch it all. Ads sports midday news your health. Adults' heads talking talking… he wouldn't say a word. A sign. Am-ma. That meant mama. Me-milk. That meant he was hungry. Ma-me – ma-me. That meant he was starving. Ba-ba. That meant "more".

If there were babies on the screen he would giggle… And then his face would darken… Suddenly. Tears would start running down his cheeks. He would start crying, Victor. He doesn't whimper – he cries. He's sad. I can see it… I can see it coming this sadness. He cries without cringing, like a man. He's tired Victor. His mother and all. Sadness… Tears running… He doesn't scream. Not loud no, but they can't stand it. They look at me askance. He tortures him the pervert! All the more – he lives with two whores… Ha ha ha… He's sure milking it! Fucks both! Suckles two cows that calf!

They can kill you the good people. He's light-hearted? Let's do him in! The bastards… They would wipe you out in no time… They belch fart but that's OK… Envious! They get drunk but that's fine! They are lewd but – it's US! Us, moron! We are local! Our shit doesn't stink! Get it? They would cut off your fingers, the righteous. They would let you die, the good- righteous. In the street. Under the blazing sun. On the footpath. The righteous. They walk past… Walk away… Neither remorse nor regret. Good riddance. We have to leave. I carry him on my shoulders. Dare-dare! Get a move on! I'm your camel! He laughs. Dare-dare! I taught him that. He likes French. We bounce around like crazy and I sing.

Valentina she stays put. She takes clients in our room. She does blow jobs, she prefers, it's a quickie. She knows how to speed it up. To slow it down. She can make you see red sails and then the sea. She never undresses from the bottom. The top first… The blouse the jumper all that… Stilettos, tights and the rest of it. She walks around in all her shameful splendour. Slow, she smokes.

She tells me. How. She's a pro in bed… No guy can resist her tongue. She makes them miaow after just one minute. She experiments. She holds her breath and – silence. One minute… She tells me!

---It's the first assault that counts ---And then ---He sees his own soul in red! ---The first movement and – he empties his mag! ---

She's lying in mountains of sheets. Her gear is ready. All she has to do is spread them – the wet fire leaps up. The guys sniff and enter. I can see them through the walls. The last one leaves around 2 p.m.

The camel and Victorius come back to the hotel. I bring him back on my back and I hear rrr rrr in his tummy. He's hungry. We come in noiselessly – the mother is sleeping. Once on the floor he goes to her. He crawls crawls so fast – but he doesn't touch her, no. Doesn't wake her up. He stops and grabs the edge of the bed. One hand… Then the other. He is standing. He is looking at her… Looking…

Cooking in the rooms is forbidden but we don't give a damn. We cook. For Victorius. Afterwards I open the window. The girls bribe the landlord but still… I'm a local, yes, but they have all forgotten me. About me – they know nothing. It bugs them… I'm a shady character. I don't sip a beer walking in the street. Weird that guy. Half dumb half mute. Always thanks. Weird… Trafficking organs maybe… Buying… Selling… Hearts… Lungs and all. Watch out!

He loves pasta Victor and it's lucky, yes, because it doesn't smell.

A lullaby… Dare-dare! Too-ra-loo-ra! He wants me to sing. Alright. I rock him. He falls asleep quickly his mother laughs ---You too ---You have a way with language ---Look how he *plonk!* and snoring ---You have a trick---
He falls asleep his face open like a full moon. I stay in the room. I sing sing… The girls are sleeping too. I don't stop. I keep humming. I feel lonely. Even if a singing man is never alone – I feel lonely. I sing, I don't stop! To be even lonelier, even more so. He has to teach me. Yes. Victor… He has to teach me how to cry… Like him.

I think of my son, of you my little feather, my bear cub… Sonny. So far from here. Far away. Two hands on the map between us. Life… I look at the walls of this room. This hotel… My life. I look at the wallpaper. The flower pattern…

Not closing my eyes. I just have to keep singing softly. Very softly… On the other side of life…
Sometimes we sing all together. With the girls… "When the party is over". Their favourite. They all sing. Damiana Valerie… Even Nadia… We listen to those Parcae Victor and I. Our bellies full. On Sunday… Our bellies are full on the weekends. To throw up…

---Love… On my last sunset all I shall see will be love. Oh my sisters! It's a party. Love is a party where we go together and come back alone. All we can do my sisters is sing very softly. And men all they have left is hate they die they leave us alone my sisters… the party was beautiful. Beautiful… And the end will be long girls. When the party is over. When the party drops like the wind – it's the end… When the party is over – we'll pick the corpses of flowers. We'll pick the shadows… My sisters… Shepherdesses of shadows---
I'm tugging at my ear. Victor is snoozing. They don't like it the girls… the guys snoozing while the girlies are singing love. They hate it. We'll have no ballads anymore Victor… Watch out!

I look at Damiana. She's listening with her head slightly tilted… As if she was putting on an earring. She's coming back little by little. From the country of that song. Those savages, the Russians, they are good at it… The convicts' songs and all… It squeezes tears out of your whole body. Out of your eyes. Your skin. It squeezes out sweat. And the heart. The song over – you're naked. Head between the legs, your soul bare.

Yes Damiana, yes. Yes. Love and death are next-door neighbours. But it's death who's the landlady. When death gives you the rent bill… You pay up… You can't say no to that lady. Yes Damiana. Yes. A woman who sings love – sings shelter. The man sings only death.

Entertaining them… They ask – France. France! Chanting in unison like Roman matrons screaming "Death! Death!"
Especially at night. They were bored the girls. France… Go on… More! More!
The first nights it was starting with this word. Frantzyia. They were so tired… Then it was Paris. I was telling them… Until the silence, the silence when people open their hearts… Women are truly generous only with children and convicts. With a stranger. The farther away you come from – the more fascinated they are. The rest of it is just commerce.
I've come from far away. From Paris. I was let's say refined… I was not drinking at all, not swearing too much, not spitting on the ground. I wasn't talking like I was from here. The guys here talk in slow motion… I was offering them my hand when they were getting out of a taxi. Simple spaghetti I was eating them Italian style. They thought it was funny. With a fork and a spoon. I could cook up something… from nothing. From three grains…

On those nights I told them about the sea… Saint-Malo. The northern coast… Fécamp… Cabourg… The colours of that sea. The winds. Then – the Atlantic… Rochefort…

Above Paris… We would fly… Place Clichy… Caulaincourt… Montmartre. My quarters… boulevard Rochechouart. Barbès… And then further, yes, beyond the bridges all the way to Stalingrad. They were amazed at that. Sta-lin-grad?!!!
Then a flutter of wings and we glide towards the park of La Villette… The canals.
Those night flights… It was beautiful… Sometimes I was switching to French not noticing. They were listening saying nothing dreaming. Nights were passing quickly before their wide-open eyes. And I – I was speaking in silence. It wasn't a big deal. But the voice… It's the voice that matters. Always. Only the voice. A voice in the night is worth its weight in gold. I was speaking softly… Very softly. A voice coming from far away.

But one day the kid gets sick. I went crazy. I was alone and I was going nuts. I was rocking him… He's going to die! Die… The worst! I always imagine the worst. That's why I'm such a good prophet. But he was so sad… He wasn't playing, wasn't smiling, at all… looking straight ahead… Staring… For a moment. Then closing his eyes. He had a fever, the kid. He was burning. Angina. A bad fever. I was freaking out! With him in my arms I was rushing about like a roach when the lights go on. A doctor… Closed. Another one. But it was a she and heartless. Wouldn't even touch him. Then another one who asked if I was his father. I say – yes. Yes, fucking yes! Holy Jesus! He asked his age. I said ten months. He put him on the scales. Victorius… So sad he was accepting everything. Everything. And that doc slow like a turkey! He thought it was funny… A sick kid! That pompous castrate – weighing your soul Victorius. He was fiddling with you for an hour that soul-weigher… He was turning you this way and that way. Finally – he got it and he gave me all that we needed oh that marvellous doctor! May St Peter weigh your soul with the most precise of scales! On the way back you were sleeping Victor. You cooled down a bit. Good… You were dripping. Sweating like a logger… But how scary your breathing… That whistling…

I was afraid of putting you into your bed. In my arms… It's safer. All day… your face so calm. With you in my arms – standing sitting lying… I was sending texts to the girls. No money to explain it properly! Not even to tell fuck you out loud! SOS texts. They came back at last… Eyes glazed… Like hens at midday.

I'm doing the cooking. Damiana… She's singing. She's cleaning and singing. To wash the floor and – sing… Singing while cleaning… To clean the tiles and – sing. To wash well, really well. Everywhere. From floor to ceiling and under the beds, low heavy beds – to wash and sing. To lean over and sing, to change the water in the bucket, mop and – sing. Then – laundry. To go out to hang it and. Sing. Awesome. Valentina is smoking in bed. She's talking. I can feel tears coming.

---He's starting to lose his mind my grandad. Old he is ninety---Imagine---He did two wars---Two! ---He survived everything---Everything and now he can't cope anymore---It's cancer---Lungs both lungs dead--- Before it was OK but now---In the morning always in the morning---He hides his head under the pillow---I listen ---It goes on my god---He can't do without an injection---He doesn't recognise me anymore---An injection! The only thing he asks for---And then he falls asleep---It freaks me out---When he calms down---When I don't hear him anymore. Is he

dead?---I wonder---I listen---I can't see if he's still here---I tell myself – it must happen---It must happen… Yes. Let him die---And then I'm happy when he wakes up. Happy---
She falls silent. Her eyes are dry. We shall see Valentina, we shall see, all, all of us shall see how we manage when death comes.

It's so slow this life here. Like a song of a blind-drunk coachman. So wistful…
Damiana… The sun is hiding. A cloud a big ball of grey wool is floating there. Damiana… The sun will come back. It always comes back in the south. And you – you're the South, Damiana…

I would like to turn you into a cat. A witch cat. You would see things that men can't see and you – you would tell me.
But the beaches Damiana… The beaches. The beaches of my torment… I was waiting for you here, in the sands, exhausted, like a mad monk, a debauched monk I was watching out for you… I wasn't undressing. No bathing. To become invisible, to become an eye and to see. Gloomy I suck the blood out of the others, here, I suck them dry all that are here men and women, each body each movement each glance.
Look there… Look! Don't look away. Keep your eyes on them! There! And see… Watch them, there, on the sand… These nude gods, these young gods, their faces turned up to the sun, eyes closed. Yes, but you, don't close yours… Watch. The heart of life is here. Look into it. The two-thousand-year-old heart is throbbing… Here. Everything happens here. Gods are resting in this invisible circle. Indifferent. Stretched out like at the bottom of the ocean. And

the girls… The girls, these young fishes, curious, these fishes envious of that strength… They roam around… For centuries and centuries. It's been two thousand years… Nibbling at your glances, but it isn't you, no, it's them, yes, those are their real prey. That somnolent trinity… Those three… And you – watch. Watch… Everything is here. The heart of life is fluttering… Here, on the sand. And the sun is so strong… Now, it strikes everywhere, it tracks you to death… It's forging the sky, and it tolls noon. Moans. All is bright. All is naked… Watch… And stay here.
Damiana will come… With her you will live those two thousand years again. Again. Here. On this beach. You will see it all again. This infernal machine will roll over you… Will crush you again. Once more. And you Damiana, you! She'll be here, with the fishes who circle those three… She will be here, at a whisper's distance from me and she will be far away… Far! No, Damiana, we'll never leave here, we stay. I would like to see everything… Everything. To become sober from suffering. Sober… Everything will happen here. Everything is here. The rest is just palliatives, yes, for the old days. For the agony… To have it mellow I hope. Like wax.

No one here. Only us. We are alone. You and I… I lose all sense of myself. Resurrected dead I touch your hair.

The night piles us in the room. I sleep on a mattress. Victorius snoozes on his small camp bed like a soldier. He snores… So exhausted. He collapses and then silence. Around 4 a.m. he emerges. Hello Your Snoring Majesty! For the rest of the night he plays trumpet with his nose. Eyes open my night goes by. At dawn Victor ejects himself from the bed and there it goes at a trot for the rest of the day. This kid – like a cucumber, he grows in his sleep. Bright-eyed and bushy-tailed – in the morning he wants to go out. Ramble Dim! The forest… The parks. The beach. The sand. I teach him how to swim. In two months he will swim like a dolphin, the kid. We paddle we duck we come out bouncing. Getting the water out of the ears. Right foot – left foot! We smudge each other all over. Ramble Dim! We'll rest in the coffin – come on, let's go!

The girls sleep. Well. Valentina laughs in her sleep sometimes. Lucky her. The Queen of Balls… Late to bed and late out. Hanging around with her eyes closed until noon. Then – it starts all over again.

This bird… It suffers. I wake up in the middle of the night. It has lost its nestling. It cries and cries resigned to its loss. So much despair there… Its laments bounce off the walls and fly into the darkness, then I hear them in the distance. It comes closer the bird. Resigned to its loss but searching… Then it goes away again.

Evenings – it's life in whispers. Victor's sleep. Big snooze. It's sacred. We switch to whisper. We live hushed. Then we fall silent altogether.

I get up to pee. I drag myself in the dark. The toilet – at the very end of the corridor. The lost bird falls asleep… That poor soul collapses somewhere. Hides. In the grove yes, somewhere in the night.

Back in the room I look at Victor for a short while. Very short. If he is alright. His face. If he's well tucked in… All that…

I turn around and – I see the girls. Their faces in the night… Almost unfamiliar. It makes me wistful. I fly over the dark cities. Abandoned cities. These girls' faces. It makes me fly… Fly over ghost cities. In the cold I fly, in spirit, like a dead man I fly I feel nothing not the night not the cold not anguish… And I come back here. I'm cold. Nights are warm, and I'm cold inside, cold.

I go back to bed. Listening to their breathing, Victor's and the girls' – I fall asleep. It's my family here. Now. A mirage… For a short while. Very short… For a little pinch of life it is here my family.

I started to forget my dead. Face after face. Sorrow after sorrow. From one agony to another – I forgot them all. My son… My little feather! And I had Victorius on my hands. Him on my back. Victorius this, Victorius that.

Damiana… We were making love day and night, twisting in frenzy, two worms in the soil of spring eternal and I forgot everything. In flesh and in blood – I forgot everything. Everything. I was feeling light and I was heavy so heavy. I was at the bottom. I slept better than a thousand-year-old oyster and I ate well. Living in Gloryhole, I was – arse here and dick in paradise. I forgot death.

The whole of the Far East was on fire. The Urals' forests, the taiga, even the Mongolian steppe. They were talking about spring being too hot. Not a drop and the wind. The wind… Not a spit since April and now it's June. Nothing like that for the past fifty years – they were saying. And it was going on and on… Fires were roaming around. The Volga smelt of stale smoke. Like a cold sauna.

The Volga, our hair, stones, our clothes, Victor's head – all smelt of smoke. Damiana… The smoke is floating, but you are swimming. You dive under the smoke. I follow you – your path underwater. It's long when someone is underwater. You search and she swims… Swims…

Days were passing by. We weren't even talking anymore. She was swimming in the mist… The forest on the island opposite was emerging from the fog. Like a haunted castle. She was swimming in the tepid waters. – Come, she would wave to me and I would enter the steaming waters.

Get out! Get out of me! She was shuddering. Her body. All over. She… Get out of me… Her eyes dying. She expires in whispers… Come here! In the water. Here… I want you to come here…
Fish… Slowly… They have come. To feast… Venus… This short strand of sperm. They shredded it. There… They ate the dancing sperm… We were there, both of us there, she and I and we watched the fish eating the sperm… It went on for so long… So close to us the old world was hungry. Always hungry.
Coming out of the water I touched the ground. I have to die. Yes, I understood I had to die each time. If you can die… Then, on this bank facing the black water – you will be alive. Alive… That's why I touched the ground. And I saw my shadow splitting into three.

She was bringing waterlilies. From a good distance. Long stems. Long… In her mouth. She was swimming like a long replete reptile. I was making waterlily crowns. Garlands… She was wrapping herself into the blanket. Absent and alone, yes – a mummy that was waiting for its day to come.
Making garlands I was thinking of my son. Him… How I used to sew for him. To patch up his clothes. To repair his woollen socks, to sew his buttons. I was walking far away I was looking at my hands breaking the stems. Gently all by themselves.

Nothing but the black waters of the Volga. Those heavy waters… And before me its deep bed opened up. Like a Parca I was… Weaving garlands. The waterlilies, their flowers fresh cool at first – turning dry.
She's here Damiana. She's my heart and the nail… To be near. Very near her soul. Her face… To see it… Her cliffs her hills the river of her mouth. To be nothing. Dust. To become eyes… And to look. To see… This country… To become blind to see what never dies. In the country of her face.

Damiana… Like a chrysalis she lies dormant waiting for her day to come. I, who am I here? By this body enshrouded up to the eyelashes. Who am I…
I hear a chant. Every morning I listen to this chant… It comes from the islands… They appear out of the fog, flooded with spring, and – they ascend… Every day they ascend. Islands dipped into the troubled waters of the Volga – they show up. Trees grow out of the water… I see the forest coming out of the river. Three big islands appear out of the mist. Every day… Every morning I see them growing.
I'd forgotten these islands. I'd forgotten the spring of this place. It was so long since I was here last. I'd forgotten them, these islands. I'd forgotten that it was so wide this river so deep and these islands… The forests coming out of the cold water.

And this chant… Every morning it wanders here. From one island to another. It slides closer on the surface of the river and then – no, it goes away. Far away again. In the mist… Every morning I guard this body, and this chant – it comes closer…
She's sleeping Damiana. I slip noiselessly towards the water, not even breaking a single blade of grass – I crawl towards

the water. I enter this steaming river and I swim towards this chant. Towards the islands… It's far yes, it's soon – I see them, they are coming… They are nearly there the islands. Just a little more and – I'll be there. They are already taking over the horizon. Solemn islands. And the trees, I can almost discern them. Covered in silt, black they are glistening… A little more… I swim swim… And I go back. Always I turn back. I always come back. I crawl out of the water exhausted and collapse. Nothing will make me move again. A little more, yes, before I fall asleep I hear that chant again and then – darkness.
It will drown me one day that chant. Will lure me into the mist and kill me. One morning. Towards those silent islands I shall swim without turning back. I shall swim with no chant, no breath, mad with tiredness, dazed, all the way. And there it will be – the certain end. Then the corpse, fearful they would fish me out, I would feel nothing. I will have my second baptism and I won't come back here anymore. All that, I think about all that, about the coldness of the water, about Damiana and I say to myself – one day, yes.

She was picking up a shellfish and it wasn't dead. Between her fingers I saw it – it was alive. Alive.

People they want to take everything. Everything… They want to take everything home. To leave nothing behind! Photos and pebbles – to take everything. To gobble up everything and then shit beauty.

Take everything but first snuff it – with your kodaks by the ocean in fury. A tsunami grabbing you by the balls. Dance on a volcano – photos, more, one more! To take everything. Everything. Fix everything in your dying eyes, you, immortals.

Take everything but before – become things. Let things kill you! Things you've seen, docile things kill you from a distance. All. Let the sea that is licking your sneakers go wild! Let it rage! Let the ocean the snow the hurricane break your knees one by one, your ankles, one than the other – so that you know who the boss is, the real one – before you kick the bucket. Let the matter go docile, yes, tender, but afterwards, after, let it first bring your faceless corpses to the shores, vomit it tenderly at the feet of your souls. And then we shall see, as the blind would say.

We only see dead things. Never in motion. We can't... can't see life... That moment... Life that disguises itself as a corpse and flees gently, here, there, right in front of our eyes, in front of our words.

All, all those I've known kill. More or less all. I too used to kill. I looked at things being born and dying in my hands. I saw pups children being born. I was tilting my head to see, yes, stretching out to see everything. Everything close up. Who am I to say all this, to say these things... They say – bad. They say – I don't know how to love. They say – he has no love in him. They shout – WOLF, they scream – WOLF and the wolf, it will come. Among us it will appear disguised as a lamb, a nocturnal lamb, and lie in wait. Am I a big bad wolf in a lamb's skin? The skin of my life inside out. Life? We don't give a fuck, all we want is to take our pleasure of it, again and again, safely, not to pay, and to make it last, oh make it last, and we see only dead things, frozen things. Rigid. We adore this, things that die in our hands. We live among dead things and we don't know it. We adore death, the only thing, the real thing that still makes us shiver. Really shiver, twist in ecstasy and then – nothing. That's all there is. Then – it will be out turn to snuff it, and we'll snuff it with our pockets sewn up.

Nothing to bring nothing to touch nothing to remember nothing to keep. Yes I lost everything cut off everything. No photos or anything. A few mementos and then nothing. A few little things from my son – nothing else. I'm afraid of looking at them. Afraid.

If you want to see if the girl is phony or not – take her to the sea. To a big river… Somewhere grandiose… You will see… Her eyes… Whether they kill everything they see – or not. Or not… But it's rare. Rare… Really rare. It happens once in ten lifetimes.

She – no. The Volga, the islands, she was looking at them and. Everything was alive. A shellfish she was touching it and it was alive.

I was dragging myself behind her and touching nothing. Nothing. Like a bad dog a sick dog I was dragging myself behind. And it was good yes to simply hang around that girl to see her light steps… Her footprints on the sand. Her bare feet. The sunset on her face. The marks of the evening on the skin of those who are coming back from the river… To come here when there's no one. In winter. When the fog is taking over the city. When the place shows its true wounds. You glimpse some bones on the beach. Real bones in the fog. And I will return there. In spirit.

Once we went into the steppe. Three days three nights – steppe steppe steppe. Nothing else. Freezing nights after torrid days. We slept under the four-wheel drive. It cools down slowly… We were waking up late but late. At midday. Our head in the shade, our feet at noon. It was beating down hard the sun. I was opening my eyes and seeing the grass blades trembling. They were scorpions' tails. They were hiding from the sun under our four-wheel beast. And then a snake… Just a grass snake… Between my legs…

That was my fastest waking up. Later we got a rope from the Tatars. A long plait made of horsehair. The beasts – they wouldn't crawl over it. We made a circle and crashed in the centre of it. Under the belly of our tank. Dead on our feet.

Night and its breaths. The Volga… Its blue becomes darker. I'm in a dream. I can't get myself to wake up. The shady grey and the wind. Whooo… A breath comes and goes. Goes. Water has goose-bumps. I see us me and her. Our first night. So long ago… So far… She kissed me without a word. Without closing her eyes. Slowly… Kissed me… And night fell on us.

I sit down there… My back against a big stone. Close to the Volga. Not too close no. Not too near. To stay dry. By the rocks. Grass on the left and the wind. Splash splash of the river… It's gentle here. Further away it's raging. Hitting the cliff. Those psh-sh-sh… And then it crashes. Ba-bang! It retreats… Rocks are buzzing from the heat.
To be so old and calm… Older than these waters older than these islands…

And then the smell of the sunset, the smell of the sleeping sun. And the grass almost blue. The fog spreading everywhere. The smoke of the day. The day was heavy. So tired… The smell of the soil. Fresh soil. The mist spreading everywhere. Waterlilies. Their long stems. Long… The smell of the darkness. The heart of anguish is there.

She talks to me Damiana. She talks to me in my throat. She talks to me in my head. She used to disappear but never for more than a week. I was looking for her everywhere I was waiting for her waiting. I was going back to the river bank, spending three nights wandering around and. Nothing.

She didn't come anymore, no. No… Again and again I see her hair over her face, her hair soaked with sweat.

Her tights. A fishing net. So close… And my eyes. Of her – I have only that net left. Yes, a net for catching souls. She… The soul catcher. Through this net I look at our nights. Through the squares of this net… I'm calm. I'm a fish… A soul. A caught soul. Damiana… Love made – she flies away, the little bird… Curious. She flies away then roams around naked, light, indifferent, like a cat. Smile, yes, that smile of tired pity, almost despising. She had forgotten her dead too. She forgets everything. She wipes out everything. Me, this room, my sperm that runs down her thighs, drips on the ground… I see all that. I curl up like a snake and I watch. I don't take my eyes off her. Not her face, no, I avoid it… My desire follows her with catlike stealth, I keep her in the corner of my pupil.

To pay with my life – I say. To sell myself, my skin, everything, my body, truly everything. Everything… My desires, my hearing and my tongue – everything. Put out one of my soul's eyes – for one thing, yes, only one little thing, for a magic eye that can see this girl for real. Truly. Undressed from me. Stripped naked from me. An eye that can see everything. The whole infernal machinery of it… That can look into the face of desire and not close. Never close. That can read everything and read it right. That doesn't speak… That sees in silence. To sell everything for one eye and then, blinded, to see it all, and at last, yes, at the end of it all – to board this boat that is life, to smash its figurehead that so fascinates… That leads to death with no awakening.

Damiana… You don't even look at me. You smile smile… The smile of a blissful figurehead. Did she love me? The answer will be long, long like my life and longer still. Farther still, yes I know it. I shall see it harder and harder, closer and closer that mask of desire. I shall see her lips moving. She will tell me and I will look, yes, to the very end I will read her lips. To the end. You have no love in you, you have only death in you and you're scared, scared, because dying comes ahead of loving.

Summer is there. We are on a permanent jaunt. We stroll like prehistoric men. I – I'm a prehistoric mother. I tie Victor to my back and we go deep into the forest. I walk singing, it lulls him. It's hot. Heavy… The sky becomes overcast. It smells like a storm. As a kid I could smell a storm coming from afar. Its scent… In the forest it announces itself even louder the storm. You can see something change. Change imperceptibly… It becomes a different forest.

I sing but he doesn't want… he fights sleep. The forest distresses him. He doesn't want, Victor! He doesn't close his eyes. He doesn't cry he hangs onto me he clings. Once he nearly strangled me. My neck compressed I saw the stars and then he let it go. He got frightened. He was shaking… The forest, yes, it's this forest… I knew it well – we used to play here, when I was a kid and I was the king of it. I could hide better than the others I was never ever scared here. With my mother we used to come here. As soon as we entered it her face would change. Barely recognisable she would become but I wasn't scared. She would drop my hand. She would go farther yes, deeper into the shadows, always deeper. I would follow. She would sing softly and. I would follow her voice. In the forest she would talk little. She was never turning around to check on me never turning her head. She would keep humming in this enchanted forest and her voice would guide me.

It's the first time since her death, with a child on my back, that I come here. I didn't know yet what I was looking for in that forest. I don't know that I'm chasing a spirit. A ghost. With a child on my back. In this enchanted forest I am looking for the trace of a spirit. Yes. My eyes my heart my soul wake up…

Every day we come here. We go deeper and deeper into the forest and. Step by step in the shade in the most silent shade I understand. Why my eyes are rifling through the ground… I understand… Carrying this child on my back… I'm chasing a spirit… A she-demon that will change my whole life. A she-ghost that will take my heart, my blood that will leave my soul homeless – wandering. Roaming day and night in this forest, in the faraway cities, the big cities… Amid the murmurs of languages… Among other souls. A she-demon that will be by my side. Always there, day and night I shall feel her presence. In the deepest roots of my veins. She will be in my breath. She will become my respiration in the calmest hours of the night when the night falls asleep with the baby dawn in its arms.

Before the storm… Victor fell asleep on my back. He nodded off quickly. He was becoming heavy but heavy in his sleep! It was strange yes, how he dozed off. Usually I would rock him as I walked for hours… But this time…

When light rages in your pupils. When noon crushes them. I don't wear sunglasses. I don't blink. That's how you make out the dead from the living. In broad daylight. At the height of it.

The hour of the dead and the midday sun are setting my shirt ablaze. The white lashes of the sky. Matte heat… The nakedness of the sky… Milk poured into its blue. Heat… This hour of the dead and their road. So long… The heat of their midday meal. Invisible is their fire. And shadows are celebrating their wedding. That hour… The nuptials of noon.

The storm. It's coming… The sky is drunk. Drunk! And furious. It spits on the ground. And its first spittle brings ashes back to life. The strange scent of the dust, the old scent. The scent of open graves.

We got farther deeper into the forest. The storm and Victor on my back – I almost ran. Yes, farther. To the deepest of the forest. It welcomed me with open arms and I reached a place where no noise could be heard. Not a sound. Not the storm not insects not leaves. Not the wind. Not a breath and there I stopped… Damiana… Lying down under an apple tree. With a guy… Both asleep. There. Both of them. Like dead.

Damiana… Damiana… I switch to French. To impress her! I have trouble with Russian, I have no more warmth, no more curses. Like a fool, yes, anything – to make her laugh, to make her smile. All my blood… Let it rave.

And there – the door opens. Victor! I calm down, I stop… Buffoon…

Tied to a chair – I'll end up. One evening. Myself – I'll tie myself. She'll go to the forest. With one of those guys – yes, with one of them. I'll tie myself tight with Sellotape. Well wrapped around. Victorius will hang around surprised, a new game? He and I we'll stay in that room. Us. He and I… It calms me down a child.

Not to run in this forest. Not that… Not to see them. Her and him – no. Not to kill them… They're so close so deaf from pleasure. Deaf! And then… Tied up – I'll close my eyes. I'll invoke the spirits. The bad spirits. Let them come from all the corners of the world – let them come. From the earth and the air…

I want someone to come. To kiss me. Man woman whatever… A child. Kiss me. Touch me. Quite simply yes – just touch me. Anyone…

I know this – one day I won't see her anymore. A mirage… I'm dazed. This dream will stop one day, will disappear. All of this… This bucolic life… This room. Victorius Damiana Valentina. The girls… The rest of it. The walls of this hotel, the flowers on the wallpaper. Everything will fade away. Everything.

Dazed. I watch and I'm dazed.

And on that night… Precisely on that night my nightmare will come back more terrible than ever. Always the same. I dream… I'm in the snow. I'm in the army. Yes in our army lost in the Arctic.

I'm alone and the snow is charcoal black. A snow drunk with the encounter. Every other night I have this dream… The eternal encounter… And then I feel it. That bear, in my sleep I feel it, it's there. I don't see it, I feel its presence. I hear its heavy breathing. Calm… The old breathing of a demon. I wake up soaked in sweat. Dripping, my hair drenched… I stutter from fear…

But I know. I know it – one night we'll meet. I will see it face to face. And I won't wake up. It will come out of the night in all its splendour. I will see it close up… It will come closer. Slowly it will come towards me. So slowly as only happens in nightmares. There is no fear greater than the fear I will feel. At that moment we'll be face to face. Eyes into eyes. I will not wake up again. We'll be there…

the two of us he and I and my body dead from fear. We'll be motionless he and I. In this black snow empty of all breathing we'll be face to face. It will look straight into my eyes. Straight into my soul. It will search my soul. A warm soul a furtive soul…
In the night he and I we'll be alone. It will be everywhere that old night of fear. And I will see the darkness turning into light. It's there – that black light and this demon who at this moment is looking straight into my eyes. Who won't let them turn away. Before this demon of the cold… Just before dying I will see. Myself. I will see myself in this demon. I will walk into this black light and. I will wake up dead. Without realising. I will rove for nights years looking for the one who will tell me of my death. That I'm dead. Dead, and my death isn't life. And the winter will be long.

It was two deserters who saw him. They said – yes, we saw him roaming around… They ran into him during their escape. Far from the lights, far from the yurts, far from any human breathing. He was wandering around his mug bloodied. His head heavy… He was shaking his head. He didn't touch them. And then, they got it. Both of them at once – they understood that it was fucked. He made them enter his kingdom. They got it then – there will be no return. They will be hunted to death. The manhunt had been open. Then they understood that they were already dead. He looked at them unblinkingly. Smelt them… For a long while he observed them… Time stopped. And then he left. A demon doing his night round. A demon king. He dives into the ocean… Swims. Swims… Melancholy. Then comes out. Day and night he roams ceaselessly. Walks. Walks… No one had seen him sleeping. Lying down. No one had seen him hunting. The blood on his mug seems eternal.

Soldiers were disappearing. Dogs… A hunt came to nothing. Choppers, snowploughs and all… Nothing. He was turning black at night. He was turning white on the snow. A demon… The Yakuts were saying – it's an old demon. They were praying praying… They were making their shamans rich. The shamans they were drinking up to the back teeth. True sponges. Even their reindeer stank of booze. They were intoxicated to death the reindeer. They were chewing their harnesses.

And he the demon was still showing up here and there. He was coming out of the night like a black light, that bear. The officers didn't believe it but people were disappearing day after day… Everywhere. On the way to the canteen. At night. When the northern lights were raging. Gods are having orgasms in the sky – the shamans were explaining, belching.

People were disappearing the nights when gods were dozing and in daytime when the snow blinded even vixens. The young… the old… the women… No bodies or traces found. He was taking their souls. Not the body not clothes not a grain of blood.

The missing were in the middle of a nightmare and they weren't going to wake from it.

I'm not a soldier anymore. I say – it's over and – no, Dim. Not to her not to anyone… And before – to nobody… Telling all this. My North… The army… I was scared. Some were still alive, I was afraid they would come to see me, the survivors, one by one, and then in a circle, to sew up my peepers before killing me. And at that point – I open the graves.

III

I'm not a squaddie anymore. It's been a long time... The army of shadows... It was in a different country. Far from here in the snow. Ten fingers from here on a small-scale map. At the Pole.

Yes, I say – the Army... All the snot. All the spittle of the country. Former cons, small-time thieves, morons, paranoiacs, chickenshit... Bedwetters... There were even two guys who had only seven fingers each. That gang... All of us on that ship... But I'm Bruegelising... There were a few who had never set foot on a boat. It was throwing up in every nook and cranny. I slipped on vomit a few times. Like a pig our lieutenant snores and chucks it up too. It smells of rotten food. We slip, we fall, we vomit on each other... We shake. Eyes bloodshot.

A ship full of fools. We move on... The shore is far away. But we can still see it. We can still make out things. The last glimpse of the shores before the ocean. People there... So small... And then we get closer. Women doing the washing. The small piles of laundry behind them... Like dirty snow. We can even see their faces... The ship moves on... They all stand up straight. Their faces for a second... Their eyes following us. A second... Slowly. And then nothing. We get farther and no more faces. The Lena River becomes wider. Out of sight... Out of everything.

When the ship leaves the delta of the Lena… The Laptev Sea receives us in silence. On the river – a hell of a noise. The noise of ice scraping the sides of the ship. Sighing moaning ummm ummm! Big chunks of ice knocking rapping the tired ship and plunging back into the muddy waters of the Lena. And suddenly – nothing. Nothing. A great silence. We come out into the open sea. We hear nothing anymore. The ship moves in silence… In slow motion. In a dream slowly among floating ice – we move forward. This silence… The young sky shuts up the heart. The soul is dizzy. And then the cold mist… Suddenly. Out of nowhere. Everything turns white as far as the eye can see. I can barely see the faces. We drift in silence… This ship full of soldiers in the fog. A ghost ship. And us… Revenants. An army of ghosts. It will go on for two years. Two endless winterings. Two years to drink the ocean and piss it back.

Frozen ground. Perennial frost and – we were digging… A labour of Heracles? He, Ajax, son of Telamon, Achilles, Ulysses – the whole gang of them – could have done nothing! Scratch the slate. Scratch with your index finger! Nailsuckers! That frost… Virgin for millions of years! And us poor wankers – we were tapping at it tapping at it… We were preparing the ground. For the airplanes to land! My arse! It was already flatter than Versailles' Royal Table! But keep digging soldier! Keep digging. Scratch the eternity. Those labours are still waiting for their Homer! The hot body of youth…
With a shovel. An old woman – a hundred-year-old Yakut – our Helen of Troy.
Our Agamemnon it's the colonel. His screaming I hear it even in Paris.

---Fuck each other like I've fucked you! Faggots!---Fairies!---I'll teach you how to piss standing!---
War, my arse, we won it and why did we beat the Fritz?---We were eating rats!---The Fritz wouldn't eat rats or cats---We were crashing in the snow and falling sleeping!---No flu! We were eating soil and we have won! And you! No balls!---The war, its name is FOREVER!---You aren't going to get bored here---The war is still on!---The war and the boredom---I've made my choice---And you too---My soldiers! My sissies of a bitch! ---The war or the boredom! ---

Brrr! The pores of my skin are shutting down. I can hear him from here our colonel. The last Great War, he was there alright, the vampire. Wounded ten times he survived. He showed us the scars in the sauna. He was strutting his body… A shapeless rock full of crevasses. His scars! Fat earthworms. Pink. Moved.
---Rub yourselves!---Come on clowns! Perform your ablutions well!---Mouths!---Louse, it hides everywhere!

His soul, yes, it stayed there, near Stalingrad, he left it near the Volga. It flowed out of his body through the ten holes. It is roaming there…
I have to be careful when I return – I was saying to myself – I have to watch out.

Tundra tundra… Your carpet strewn with flowers… A thick carpet. And the flowers… Small. Tiny. Smaller than the eye of the needle. Colours… From green just-born to pomegranate-seed red.

The soil of my North. What could a drop of hot blood do against the eternal frost…

All those who lived through that would carry that frost in their blood. All those who survived and those who – no, the dead, buried there will remain mute, will remain young. Eternal youth in the ice. Near Tiksi. In Mirny… On the shore of the Laptev brothers' sea.

The other dead… Those who were brought home. To their land… To their villages. To their towns… If they tell the local dead about those two years… They wouldn't believe them and nobody. Nobody would.

In those places where their mothers' screams are still floating. Yes, from one house to another… The women have become old. And their gardens are ablaze with green. So fertile the lands of the dead.

And the pittance? Not bad. There were even eggs. It was Sunday the eggs day and we were getting excited about it starting Tuesday.

Bread… At first all-you-can-eat. Bread flowing like water, then – nothing. One morning – no more bread. Only one mug of coffee. No sugar no bread no milk. No bread – no crumbs. Less food – less filth. That… We swallowed it lightly at first. Alright. One morning… But no, it was going to last. Last.

Hunger. We soldiers would plunge into the third circle of hell. Night after night we would descend… Little by little. Step by step. The dogs the cats would disappear. Everything, yes, everything hot-blooded – would disappear.

We'll be the only ones on the frozen ground. We'll become the demons of these lands. The demon soldiers. The only ones hot-blooded. Red-blooded. The lonely. Ones.

Poor! Poor beast… Relentlessly we tracked her. No respite! In a pack. Like wolves. Surrounded her! A real

science… The wisdom of survival. Of wolves. Like young wolves we hunted her. To the end. Until she collapsed…
It wasn't a Pekinese! A German shepherd. A true one. A very intelligent bitch. Nervous. But there… There was nothing she could do. A pack of soldiers… A pack of men… Nothing she could do. Run… Yes. She ran. Ran. It went on and on! Bloody hell, it went on… Hours of hunt! The bitch… Seven starving soldiers! Seven soldiers mad from hunger… Ravenous like wolves. Seven young men and the bitch… Imprudent. Her instinct betrayed her. Betrayed she was doomed. Could she have fought? A dog that had a man as a master can do nothing. Nothing against a man gone mad – nothing.
We finished her like barbarians. Two penknives, boots and sticks. She wanted to hide, she was too scared, she found a crevasse but no – too small… And then – she turned around. Yes. To fight the last battle? To sell her skin dearly? No… She crawled towards us. Her tail between her legs. Like a pup she crawled… Crying… My blood. She was crying… Her eyes! To live! She wanted to live! Live…
Mad. We were mad. All... Triple mad. From our rotten soles to our heads. And above… Above. The air and the snow! Everything had gone mad. We plagued everything. And everything we contaminated was watching us… We felt a chill in our stomachs. Afterwards we walked without talking. Without looking at each other. Each was carrying a piece of the flesh of that bitch to gobble up behind the barracks.
I don't know how to say death in Yakut. We shit in our pants to keep warm. Warm yes. To keep the arse warm. We would shit and it would keep us warm the shit. We

would stay like this for a few days covered in shit. Until shower day.

We had nothing to eat, but really! Nothing to chew, only some soup. Soup. Just salty water. It was flowing fast through our fangs. Weren't we handsome. You would think Death let us out for a pee. We were almost crawling. And yet – we were getting boners. All. Ancient Greece-style erections. We could wear them for a few hours. Right at the North Pole! No beach. Neither beach nor girls nor bare skin. No. One. A hundred-year-old woman. We had boners to make our flies smoke. Her arse in view – we were lifting tables. The only one she was. Otherwise – nothing. An erection without a woman… It's a mirage so it is. A mirage of a watchman who shouts LAND! LAND! The watchmen in our pants were screaming – WOMAN! WOMAN! We had cannons on parade between our legs. The dick in the skies, pals.

She was recalling things… She was raving in the kitchen. In the middle of the soup. Whispering curses in Yakut, her loose hair down to her bottom – she was screaming syllables! In trance she was sybilising. Prophesying. Spitting into the soup – she was showing us her arse! Hairy! She peed right there in the kitchen. Standing. The golden liquid was spreading… Dripping… And she was standing there. Proud! In the middle of the golden puddle… Eyes wide open. And a smile… Yes. Her smile… Her! Joyful in that puddle, like a sea lion in a circus.

She could froth for a long time, but not indefinitely. She would crash on the floor and we could go eat our soup. Her ecstasy number ended – she would become melancholy. The comb out… She would start combing her hair

and us we would not exist. She would sing and we would enjoy the show lapping the soup.
She would comb... Her filthy hair... Worn-out threads... A crazy Parca in that big canteen. Sun-lit canteen... Her eyes observing us through her hair. Eyes of a trapped animal... Ambushed... She reminded me of my mother, she combed her hair like that, my mother. Hair brought down in front of her face and eyes watching through the grey hair... I was waiting for that moment. I was watching her. In the canteen. Eyes into eyes... From her to me. At each meal – the same. As if she could reveal my fate to me. I wanted to read it... To read my fate in her eyes... To escape it.

She also worked for the hospital. One day we'll met face to face. Yes, there. At the hospital. She will be closer. She won't be laughing anymore. She will give me fags. I will see her washing the dead. Clothing them. I will see her undressing the ill. Civilians old men half-dead old men. Indifferent. They will die with a bowl of slop on their bellies, bodies stretched. And the cold slop in the bowl.
I will see her washing us. The living. Us. Soldiers. Those with frost-bitten hands. The self-mutilated. The ones who fell asleep outdoors drunk... Those who won't have noses or ears anymore. I will see her shave them. Comfort them. Give them fags. She won't comb her hair in public anymore. She will be sitting. In the end. Sitting heavily... The polar day it won't die that soon. Three more months to go. She was making holes in her calendar to mark it better. I see her again slumped. Dead tired. Tired not to be able to get up anymore. No buffoonery or hooting. She was falling asleep like that. Sitting. Hands hanging. When we are tired to death – we become ourselves. I see her... Not crazy at all.

Serious. She's dreaming. Shhh! In grace she's dreaming. Her lead hands… Grace. It's the superhuman weakness.

She will sing in Yakut. She will lull us… But I – I won't be able to sleep. We'll be six poor squaddies in the room. Sitting in the twilight she will lull us. Softly for one hour two hours she will sing… The same thing… The same chant. Amid the snores we'll be alone, she and I. I will see the lights in her eyes go off. Go off…
There I will see things. I will babble deliriously. On the walls of our room – I will see shadows pass. I will babble feverishly. The souls of the dead soldiers – they march before my eyes. Silently. And I will not know who I am. There. In a fever. Among the shadows. Who… And us? I see her again that Parca. My mother, she died since then… and. If she, yes, that lady… If she is still alive… Still. I can still see her. Twenty-five years have passed since… We look at each other the way we did before – us, from her to me eyes into eyes. She's combing her hair… Combing. The death of just one strand of hair… It's so long… So light.
Who is alive? Who? Of those who were in that army? Us at the time… And us now.

Us, we were only her hair… Of that immortal Parca. All. All the soldiers that she had seen over the years. The dawdling ones. The dead. The mutilated. The fat. The emaciated. The ones who botched their suicide attempts… All of us we were just dead strands of her hair. In that canteen. They were falling slowly on the ground. And us we were looking at her in silence. Not a noise! No breathing… And she was combing combing…

Youth, who can tame you? Yes, we were young. We had strength too much strength. It wasn't death, no.

We didn't have death in us. Not a drop. We were pregnant with danger but not with death. We – soldiers. The young squaddies. We had snowball fights. I remember! We were throwing snow at each other and ta-dah! – I'm counting the dead. Soon I'll be even older. I'll die a little more… I didn't want to count my dead, no. I don't know how I landed there.

We masturbated sitting on the bonnet of our lorries. On their long muzzles. It was quick. We were fast… Arses warmed by the cooing engines ah yes it was calm like an endless lullaby. I can see us sitting there faces up to the sky legs open wide… In a cooing silence. Prudishness is so unbearable… We were born we were alive and – we wanted to be born again and again. There, under that sky our legs spread wide, screaming, ears blocked up from pleasure – to forget yourself and to be born again.

I can see us from here. We smile, the sea – in front of us. The polar sea of the Laptev brothers.

I can see myself there. And I see the ocean in summer. Ocean of the Great North of old lead, solemn lead. It is heavy… Heavier than our sperm.
I see lumps of ice floating. Imperceptibly. Dirty…
It was in summer. Even the dead, yes even the dead come to smell the ocean. To be there. Even from far away – there we are. Maybe the old people too they need to be born again… Yes, and the dead want to be born again too.

I can see myself there. In summer… Near the sea I could see the dead coming. Mine… Grandmother my aunt two uncles… Grandfather… I saw my dead and then the others – yes the unknown dead. The dead of others… They were coming in crowds. In crowds. Mine… And there were so many others. Unknown souls. They were springing from all sides! From up above and from down below.

Ha! He's gone, him. Our beloved doc. He wasn't stupid, gone – no shit no goodbye. He felt the storm coming, the white coat! He was imagining himself the-balls-nailed-to-the-floor. And there you go – he's off! We didn't want blood, us. Grub, that – yes. Not blood. In his room we didn't want to show him his own guts. No. Sleeping tablets, just that. We wanted them so we could sleep! At last… Empty stomach for three days. Just to kip down… Not to think of grub. Sleep! At least to stop thinking. Nothing. No dreams. No balls no tits no bums. The grub… We were dreaming of it fanatically. We were obsessing about it feverishly. We weren't fucking blonde goddesses, no. The grub, just that, of all kinds and loads of it.

The first seven days – we could barely walk. We stayed in our beds. Quiet. To save our energy. They told us – Wait… It's been seven days. Seven nights.

Time doesn't flow by when you are starving. It crawls sluggishly. Day and night. To sleep… To stuff yourself with sleeping tablets and that's it. It switches off your head… To plug out of everything… I lost ten kilos. I had to hold my trousers when I walked. To the loo at least. Later on, it didn't matter. We didn't shit much. It was mainly to piss. From time to time there was one who wouldn't wake up to piss. After – yes. The piss would go cold. It would be stinking. But nobody gave a toss. It was okay…

The officers… They lived separately. In their own houses. They ate with their own wives. Fucked them. Shaved themselves. Their necks smelt of Cologne… They belched. I remember the colonel's belches. Steak and garlic. I was smiling… His face started to inflate. I had a fever. I was smiling – maddened from empty stomach. Smiling.

Stay there! All. Go out? Forbidden. We stay squeezed behind the railings. Otherwise – they shoot. And our corpses? A shallow mass grave in the eternal frost… The depth of a spade, that's all. We'll stay there for a thousand years, not hungry, not cold – we wouldn't give a fuck about anything. Resurrected we'll wake up even more handsome, guys…

I saw them… They had been laying down in the snow. Laying down for good and then passing away. They were found a long time afterwards. Yes, those who had frozen years ago… in that ground, in that eternal frost. I was with the team who de-eternalised them. Those, the old ones… Iron bars ice picks and all that… It was hard, hours and hours… Going slowly. Without damaging them… Without touching. But the fresh ones – they were just cleared of snow with wooden spades. That – it was like a dance… Easy, like unloading a lorry of feathers. The snow was so light… We were laughing yes, we saw them emerging those crowds of stiffs. Bodies appearing, hands, we were laughing less… and in the end heads and faces. We weren't laughing at all then. Their faces such calm, such peace… Eyes closed, always eyes closed… Under the snow… And then they were defrosting in the barracks. We were putting them on the floor – easier to wipe the puddles.

Hell? No it's too easy… Who knows hell? Not many of them left. The war. The war everywhere. Indochina Vietnam… Those consumed by the Great War… There aren't many left of them. They're going to leave us, they will all leave. We will no more see them in the streets. Then in the books. There will be no more witnesses. It will be over. Empty. The theatre will be empty. They are dead, so very dead already. The witness box is emptying out. The Purgatory is emptying out… And it will start all over again… We'll have war until total exhaustion. Until total extinction. Until the last drop of blood. The cells of the last man will fight and then – it will be over. Hearts livers lungs – will fight the ultimate battle. We'll all take our own lives. We'll disappear from the mirrors. No revenants no shadows. Over. The smoke will clear. The smoke never goes back into the chimney. The ultimate battle and then – there will be no men no women no beasts. The spirit won't fly over the black waters anymore.

Hell… Those two in the army. They caught hell there. A hell of a ride. Sugar cubes stuffed into the anus. To stay in the hospital a bit longer. Those two deserters… I saw them I was passing them fags. Cave eyes. Deep…

They had fun, running in the sauna, splashing foam at each other! A big sauna – just for the two of them. To run! To warm up. To spread out your body… It's so sad in the cells. To jump and to wash yourself thoroughly without hurrying. As much soap as you want. Hide-and-seek. They were running… Catch me! Like young arrows… Young fish. Joyful.

I saw them and I see them. Still. Through a small window I see them laughing. Yes. Laughing! Naked they throw foam at each other. They slip! Through the window I see them dancing! Their racing about… A dance. In slow motion I see them waltzing. Tomorrow… They will leave tomorrow. A military prison, there goes your dance… Destination Chita. The waltz will be over.

I see them from here, and so clearly, I see them from my garret room… Dancing. Death was watching them too.

In slow motion… From the outside. Without touching them. Watching the waltz die. Another spin. Let's waltz! We watched them Death and I – dance. Dance...
Tomorrow they will leave. Dust will fall back on our boots. The day will be over at dawn.

They wanted to hide with the Yakuts. For a while, to let it blow over. They had frost-bitten hands, frozen hands. Black. In the sauna they screamed in pain. They were hurting them horrendously those black hands.
Nikita whispered to me… In the sauna he whispered to me I'm not scared no not scared for myself but him… Andrey… He's scared. He can't cope anymore… He won't last two minutes in prison. There… We have to stay in the hospital. Here. Longer. Longer. One more day. Whatever… Do something. YOU CAN'T LEAVE US LIKE THIS! TO DIE. WE AREN'T GOING TO DIE! DO YOU WANT IT?! I CAN GIVE YOU A BLOWJOB! I HAVE NOTHING ELSE!
Finish me… He was whispering, very low very softly very close.

LET ME GO. We won't survive there! We'll die there… FINISH ME… PLEASE… OR ELSE – GIVE ME YOUR KALASH! YES… AND TURN AWAY. WE HAVE ONE MINUTE! ONE! THE LIEUTENANT WENT OUTSIDE… YOU KNOW HE SMOKES FAST… GIVE ME YOUR KALASH. I'LL MANAGE. SHIT! PLEASE… ONE SECOND AND THAT'S IT…
---What is it like where you're from?---It must be snowing now---A lot of snow---No?---
He looked at me dreamily. A watchful dreamer. The way a pregnant woman looks around when the baby in her belly has just moved.

---Fields. There. In my parts it's lots of fields. Fields... Fields... Nothing but fields---Now under the snow, yes---you can see far away---Far... It's been a while---
We were from the same region. We came from the same parts. From the same bank. The Volga...

I touched his hand. I didn't want him to look at me. Then – no. It'd been a thousand years since I thought of men. It'd been a thousand years since I touched a man. And then – I didn't want him to look at me. To see me...
His hand... He was strong. I felt his strength. Him. He could take me into his arms. Like a child... Carry me... From here, from this cold carry me away. Carry me far away. Far away towards his country... With slow steps. Carry me all the way to the Ural Mountains. Cross them snow-covered... With dreamy steps... Carry me in his arms towards the greenery. To the Great Russian Valley and beyond... Further away. Far away. To where the steppe begins. And before descending – he would take a rest in the shadow of the Ural oaks. Under the oaks of eternal darkness. He would doze off. I saw them those oaks, yes. A horse can find shade in the shadow of one leaf.
Our backs against the wall of oaks – we would look at the steppe. To stay – gazing into the distance.
We'd see vermillion sails. Boats... Faraway ports. We'd feel sleep coming. We'd wait for the ocean there. It's been millions of years – it left – it will come back the ocean. Waves like slow strides it will come back.

We'd stay like that. Forgetting ourselves in the night of the steppe, yes, when the sky tarpaulins the earth. Low... Low. That sky pierced with stars. Let it tarpaulin the merchandise. Let it cover us up carefully... Days and nights would pass there under the oaks. That boundary and then the great plains begin. On those shores…

And then – the beasts. The beasts of the steppe will come. By day and by night they will visit our bodies. Our eyes… Our tongues. Foxes and jackals… Crows. And rats. An army of ants would stop over to rest. Everything would be eaten. Our memories our fears our movements… Will be cleaned. Snows rains would make our bed. Wind would get into our bones. And whistle very gently…

He and I. We swapped our winter jackets. Mine was three months old. Almost new. No fly got fucked on it yet.
His – a year and a half. Thin with holes like a colander. Winter jacket made of fish fur.
---What? You're crazy!---It's your jacket! Yours! It's new---It will be dumped there! As soon as we arrive it will be dumped!---They burn the clothes there. You!---You'll freeze to death idiot!---You say? Winter?---We haven't even licked winter yet!---

Winter. Oh yes it's true. Not even touched it yet.
Hot. I was red hot… Hot. My bones… Heated white like in a forge. Faces… Lorries… Everything. Everything started to waltz. My eyes were hot. Fever! Fuck! My lungs… That's it. My rotten lungs, that's it. A stinking pneumonia. Both sides… I was limping on both lungs… At eighteen – the sixth. Bloody hell!

That dawn… I see them at the back of the lorry. They look at me. They don't take their eyes off me… As if I could have done something. As if I could have taken their place. There… And quickly very quickly it's over. They had been rubber-stamped. And sent to hell. At first the lorry was going slowly shuddering and then faster, faster and faster, like in a dream – their eyes weren't leaving me. They were going. Going. Us, we were on the threshold. Morons dolled up to make you sick. And pleased. Because it wasn't us. It was them, it was the others who were going to hell… Not us. I see us – the three of us – Balou, Lieutenant and Dim. Those in the lorry – going… Going far away. No more faces. Nothing. We can't see anything anymore. Dust. It's settling the cold dust. Earth is coming back. Very quietly… It's covering our faces. Us on the threshold… Faces aged by a hundred years.

In silence the winter dust curtain has fallen. You Dim… You should have become one of the two. The two who are going away in the lorry. Should have become them…

They have gone. He – my name on his back. And I – remaining on the threshold. Like a firing squad… I saw my name on his back move away. Draw away…

He before entering the disciplinary fortress will spend a few nights alone in the jail. Then again they will be brought to Chita. They will be washed again and will enter the courtyard of the fortress. Terminus. My winter jacket will go into the furnace. It will be burnt with a pile of other clothes. A big pile in the furnace. And the smoke going up.

Sunday will be shower day. They will wash they will cross the courtyard shaved heads completely naked among hundreds of naked men… They will wash themselves slowly… They will wash well. Without hurrying they will perform their ablutions. For the last time. It will be their last night with men. The last time for everything. Before jumping off the roof a rope around their necks. Then they will go into the courtyard again. In dirty-white underwear.

Hundreds of men in silence they will cross the courtyard again. To fall asleep in the barracks.

Two worms among others. In the middle of the night, in the deepest dead end of the night – to wake up. Both of them… At the same time. To end it all.

And afterwards… Their afterwards. I'm going to tell you their afterwards. The army knows everything about its dead. Especially in time of peace.
They were transferred to Yakutsk. First. Then to Chita. To the military prison. I had been to Chita, I know the city. In winter. Yes. Not otherwise. But in winter – it's plenty enough. Frightened little houses. Bruegelian streets and snow snow snow.

Now, it's the question of the rope. Yes, a long long rope. I don't know how they managed to pull it off there. Honestly… First, to escape. To get out… Both of them. To get outdoors together. That's one thing. The other thing – they rented a room. Not a room somewhere, no a room in a hotel. In the biggest hotel in the city. The tallest hotel in the city. I don't remember well – how many, three four six stories… I hadn't gone in. We had been in our lorries. Always in the lorries, us. We had driven by and I'd seen that hotel. Flat roof.

On that roof – they ended their trip to the military prison. In the morning they went all the way up. Tied themselves together… Two slip-knots around the necks and a long long rope.

They ran in opposite directions. Both of them – they ran on the roof to the edge. To the edge and then – they jumped.

The head is torn off the body and does yo-yo in the air. Flies… The rope was long… Two heads were hanging there

on that morning. It was biting cold. Two heads tied with a rope. Two corpses were found far, as far from everything as possible. Projected far – their bodies… Gnawed on by stray dogs.
Out of the question – sending the bodies like that. The colonels the majors that whole gang – they decided to send the heads. Those two heads. To their families. Two heads. One was for Moscow. The other for Arkhangelsk. The city of archangels – it means. One is for the West. The other for the North.

When I see stray dogs… Those two soldiers I think of them. Two spirits that are erring. They loved each other those two soldiers. They loved each other and – deserted it here. Now the two spirits roam in search of their heads. One is in the soil of the West. The other sleeps in the ground of the North. Near Arkhangelsk. The city of archangels.

When you can't take it anymore you say yes to death. You go under the ground. Yes to the darkness. Deserting… To be born again at the moment of death. To the end of sorrow, to the end of the rope that will stitch our mouths and then – it will be all over for good.

I will wear his winter jacket until the end of my service. And every day every morning in the hospital and after I will make a hole with a needle in my little calendar. Like everyone else. There, at the Pole, on those spellbound shores, like all of us – I'll be counting my days. Through a needle hole every morning – I will see the little light. There, I was just beginning… There will be no end to it.

When a man can't take it anymore – he hides. Not to be. Not to be but to live… Everything stops. He curls up. He rolls himself into a ball, the man. Like a dog that can't run anymore and lies down in the snow... He rolls himself into a ball and closes his eyes quietly closes his eyes. Roar blizzard roar! Let everything crash down... When a man can't take it anymore he becomes light. And then – the man dies, and the light goes silent.

It's there in the North Pole that I started to scribble... After all that... We have seen, we have all seen Death dancing in the snow. She was inviting us one by one. One after the other, here goes another one, and then another... Guys were falling. Lying down... All that... So unreal.
I was writing down their first names, simply their first names and then how they were found. Death, I kept her dance card. Locations, villages, names of the Lena islands... stopping places, prehistoric winterings forgotten even by the Yakuts themselves... And now let the dead come in. The dead soldiers and the dogs too... Come in. Let the old demons of the Pole come and ask for their real name. Here. Now.

When you can't take it anymore you collapse. Slowly you lie down. You curl up in a ball. You hide the rest of your life that is just a ball of sadness. Very quietly in whispers things go away go away and pull us along. There, I started to scribble. I babbled deliriously. In a fever – I said to myself – I'm snuffing it. In the hospital. No kidding. I had visions. I saw the other guys. Who had died there. Within those walls. Their shadows were passing... On the walls. I was blackening the pages... I was falling asleep. The old woman would come in – turn me over – jab my arse and I would wake up. To fall asleep again. Deeper... Deeply. I was cold. Badly sown seed – I was looking for warmth. Deeper...

Faces... I started to forget them. My mother's face. My father's... Faces of those who stayed home. Far away! Faces of the living – I was forgetting them. And Babania's… My grandfather's. All. Enraged my eyes closed… At night I was trying to see them. To look at them. And failing… I couldn't see them anymore.

There. In that room full of us, squaddies – I could see everything. But not faces. Babania… I could see your house. Your windows… Everything… The walls, your bed in the corner. Mine, yes, narrow. My bed where I had felt my bones grow. Stretch. It was hurting me. Hurting! And you, you were saying---There you go you're growing up---It will be alright---

And the fretful morning… In that bed… There for the first time I had a liquid orgasm. I had sperm. Youth? Fuck it! My body of youth was hurting me. And I was growing in my sleep like a cucumber.

I could see Friend… Him… I could see your hands Babania. The soil under your nails. Everything! But not your face…

Little by little I left the realm of the gods of childhood. Then – I arrived into a dark place… Into the lands of cold and hunger.

I was babbling deliriously. The feverish seed. I was writing with my eyes closed… Hiding the sheets under my pillow. So that nobody would nick them! I was saving them for later. Yes. For the day when I would doubt – am I mad? Did I see them… Those shadows… Those soldiers that came from the other side. Their shapes… Deceitful! Came to warn me… Came to bother me in their place. To take me. Make my soul fly away! Make it leave! Make it abandon me… Make it go around this room one more time and. Leave… I was scared. A badly sown seed I was scared.

Shadows of the dead at dawn fly away. Black birds… Soul, open your eyes! You're scared! To leave… When a bird sees its own fly away – it flies away too.

A badly sown seed so I am. Let the black bird pick me up… Eat me. Take me. To a warm place. Somewhere warm… Bring me. To the merry lands. Shit me in some hot lands. In the islands of fairy-tale green. Far from this whiteness. Far! To the fat lands. To the black lands. I think of those two thousand men. There, near the ocean. Us… I saw us die. Kill each other. Go mad. Sick. Desert. I saw them cut their fingers. Break their arms. On purpose. I knew them all! Yes, all. Those who deserted… Who hid with the Yakuts. Who became animals… Living with dogs. They were saying – ANYTHING! ANYTHING BUT NO RETURN! ANYTHING BUT THE RETURN! ANYTHING BUT THE MILITARY PRISON!

Frozen hands. Rotten ears. Complete disfigurement – but no return! Anything, but not the prison. The whole death, to drink it to the dregs but NO RETURN! ANYTHING, BUT NOT THE BARRACKS! I remember those three who cut off their black ears. Their dead ears. Their noses… So that they wouldn't be recognised. They buried them in the tundra. And then foxes… Yes, they came those white foxes. In broad daylight! They unburied them…

I see them those three… Eating with the sled dogs. Fighting for a bone… Barking… Screaming from the cold. From sorrow… Going mad. Smearing shit over their faces. Roaring… Gobbling up frozen head dog's turds… Becoming part of the pack. And at night… Howling at night. Joining their souls with the choir of the pack. I can still see them.

Those who disappeared… Simply disappeared. Once out of the barracks – not a shadow not a scent. I was writing down all the names in my notebook. There in the hospital. I was filling in pages with names. Pages and pages. The names of the shadows passing on the walls. Sliding on the four walls… Around my bed. In a round dance. The other five sick squaddies slept. Deeply sown. Slept…

Alone. I was alone there. Eyes wide open I was following that parade. That dance of the souls coming from the other side. Their names… Every night those souls whispered their names to me.

Who is alive? Who has survived the ocean? Who will read what I've scribbled there? No one. From our vanished army – no one. Who remains… Who? Of those who hadn't tried to escape the fate… Who?

Pen-pusher you. You've survived scribbler… What a price… They have the right – them… To piss standing. You Dim – a deserter. Go away. Nothing you. Dust you. Spittle… You don't even exist Dim and you're happy. No balls no womb, go to the women's side. Piss sitting…

There were those who married Yakut women. Without ever returning home. Who is alive… Who? All will be forgotten. I will watch the shadows on the walls stretching. Like there in the North. Here in Paris in this tiny room I continue watching the shadows dance. Until there's only mine left. Mine! Mine – will speak.

I'm not a squaddie anymore. I did live like one, the bag and all… It's over now. It's over, my service. I thought – You've lived like a soldier and you'll die like a soldier. But no.

Without an army without a war – a lost soldier, that's the thing. And it's over now. My winter jacket… My backpack… I'm old for this. Soon I'll be even older. It's slow. If I were a doctor, a true one – I could have gone into the mill of Death… To see and to help. And now – all I can do is chew her bread.

To tell this sorrow? To whom… The true witness is mute. Without raping my throat – tell. Whisper. The commonplace is empty. Empty… Move on Dim. Move on… As for the sorrow – you have to keep silent first. It's when you fall silent that it starts. When your lights go dim. When you can feel Death. When she puts her hand over our mouths.

We don't know how to talk not to the dead not to the living. Whistle very softly… Very softly – to make them come to us… The dead. Awaken by the sorrow of the living.

The whole life – seeking… The whole life… In the dreams – seeking. Nights, days, mornings – seeking. A soul… Seeking to die and – living. Living… In sorrow. In sorrow that will be unbearable. A sorrow to sell your soul. That will halt you. And in the end… will turn you into stone and you will become heavy with all the woes of the living. The dead. Heavier than life. Heavier than the world – you will sink. Low. Low… Older than a stillborn baby. You will plunge Dim. In the lakes of tears of all the mothers of stillborn babies. You will crawl in the dry bed of the river of the dry tears of the living. You will crawl among the crowd of the dead. The sad dead… The dead who don't know they are dead… You will crawl towards the sea.

Like fish that go upstream to die – the souls go back towards the light of the nocturnal ocean. You will find that sorrow. The end. On the icy winter sand – you will find it Dim. The sorrow that will make us all reborn, yes, all – just before dying.

We move to a different hotel. No more Valerie no more Victor. I miss him and his cheeks like lifebuoys.

Clinging to my back… He must be running by now… Here we share the room with Nadia. A sinister dyke. She protects them. She's their mamka. Valerie's, Damiana's, the others'. They say she once killed a client. He came over with his pals and they take Valerie and then another girl. They stick a half-open bottle of champagne into her vagina and then open it… They killed her in the end. At dawn. And Valerie lost her first baby that night. The girls are telling… Nadia found them… One by one. She killed them all. With a knife. Into the balls. That's what the girls are saying… Their eyes were sparkling… Women admire another woman who dared… To lay her hand on a man. To stick a piece of steel into him. It's the holiest of the holy for women. To dare a guy.

She backs them up well. She protects us well, they say… Anyway we are going to leave Damiana and I. She heats up quickly Nadia.

---I can stay keen a long time. I – yes. Guys – no. They give up quickly ---I – no ---They are short-winded the guys. If it doesn't bite – they give up ---I – never ---

It's true. She never gives up. She has breast cancer. She never gives up the one to cuddle up to.

In the evenings we're alone she and I. She doesn't let me out. Or only to get some beer. There we are, she has got her booze. And there we go.

Before going out Damiana wanted me to kiss her. To hold her tight. Tight. Eyes shut… To be so close, yes – for our souls to mistake one body for another.

Ah yes! That's it! Screams Nadia – That's it! You've got your hands on her! But you will see you will see! You will pay.

That girl... In that hotel room she goes crazy. Our bed, it makes her dizzy. It spurs her. When she gets wet – she starts Cassandrising. An old wet oyster giving off fumes. Oh that ogress... She desires her wildly, Damiana.

She whispers to me she sputters to me – you! give me her heart back! give it to me! it will be all over with you soon anyway! sold out! locked! she'll come to me! you'll see! women always come to the women's side! guys go back to the guys'! you'll see... you too! you'll end up with the guys. leave her alone! she's mine! give her her soul back! leave!

Shut up Dim! I say nothing. That sinister loudmouthed shrew... Never ever does she keep it buttoned.

I'm almost scared so I am. Night is falling. She'll start roaming the room all naked – I know her. All night she'll be flaunting her oyster.

Where's she Damiana? She should have been back hours ago... when! when will she be back! when!

What a tripe soup it was. She started to rub her pussy against my elbow. Jungle on fire. It's smoking between her pins. Succubus.

You! You can't get it up! come on you and I! what are you doing with her anyway? you've two hearts now! two-hearted cunt! give me hers back!

She's losing it. Harnessing in the offing! What is she taking about... what? I don't even have a mobile that works or health insurance or anything. I don't even have a flat, my father is dying, I piss sitting into a cooking pot! Two hearts my arse! She's foaming like beer in the Sahara. She's seriously lusting after it. A taut rope – sinister lust! A taut worm. She wanted – fucking. Fucking. When the pussycat crawls – the sparrow is fucked! In a flash she took one of

her things out of the suitcase and. Slam the shower door, slam! Alright.
But that… That was just the beginning of the chapter. It began with heavy breathing. The hollering of a squashed owl. She came with a strident snore… There. As if the devil was trying to stick a flute into a she-wolf's arse.
She comes out looking like a hag, it's over. She collapses slowly, crashes down at last. Naked. In the neutral zone. Not by somebody's side. Not a woman not a man not a child not a beast. She doesn't even see me. Alone, curled up in a wasteland. Alone. Eyes far away. Far from this room, from me, from herself… She had a cooled-down face, a demon that burnt out. Eyes of cooled-down anger, she falls asleep her eyes open. Like those who are too tired. To death. Tired bare. Nudity that doesn't flaunt itself anymore. Grace… She had grace. Her face – I avoid it… Looking straight ahead. I see the reflection of that face in the window. Medusa dies down in the night. You're lost you Dim. Strayed. Good to work in a graveyard. You know that one day everything collapses. You know that and you wait… She laughs and her laugh is sad.

You Nadia find yourself another one… Find another Damiana quick. Put another girl, another Damiana on this see-saw of desire. To have them both there. To make the eyes of desire avert… To have a screen. To sharpen your claws! And then light, dancing, waltzing, all smiles on the skates of desire – slide along… Fly close without looking at them. Slowly glide on the skates of spring. The enchanted skates. Solo, tangoing, tracing a circle around, a magic circle that everyone would want to cross and. No one would enter alive.

Evening slowly floods the earth and I – I wait for her to fall asleep this woman. Lower. Let her sleep with the earth.

I wait. Let the sleep get under the lids of each tree. Under each leaf.

Cold ember… I'm getting closer. From her sleep she's watching me too. Her left eye is open. Like my grandmother in her coffin with an eye open. Nobody dared to close it.

I was looking for you Damiana. Three days three nights. I was searching everywhere trying to pick up your scent in the wind. Hotels bars beaches. They were having a laugh the people. You played a trick on me. I woke up and… nothing. No you… No clothes. You took my tatters. You vanished… So I put on your jeans and you – you had put on mine… I suppose… I see myself alone in that hotel room. Totally fucking alone. Good morning Dim.

That legend… Yes. Lovers who swap their clothes to cheat fate. I say – I will come back. You and my gems… Again and again I will come back to these lands… Patience.

And you… I put on your jeans your t-shirt and it was over. Over… No more you. Not at all. Neither Valerie… Nor Victor… No family. My little family… No more. Then – I leave. Yes. I have nothing to do here. No more. Now – Paris. It's up to you now… It's your turn. I want to tell you Damiana I say it to you very softly very gently. We'll see each other again. I will find you. Damiana…

From one life to another we'll search, us, one another. Lost in the cities we look for each other… From one city to another we look… We find each other for a moment a very short instant… To recognise each other. A short moment… We're recognising each other and again – losing in this long journey. From one death to another.

IV

She's typing my "Revenants Ball". Clara... Some nights, she can't take it anymore... "But Dim. Why all this. Tell me. That blackness, those sorrows. Your pages are black. It's black. All those dead. How to live all this. And yourself. How. To live with you. Your poor wife..."

Yes Clara... Yes. I'm heavy like a thousand bidets, my ecstasies are jealous, heavy, I'm a blocked bidet in ecstasy. To be light. When you can't take it anymore... When you really can't take it anymore – you become yourself. Clara. Don't take me for one of your horses of the Apocalypse. I'm only an ass, a heavy, heavy ass that hasn't shat in centuries. I'm alive. I feel like I'm becoming a shadow... Small step by small step. I, you, that whole army of people... By small spoonfuls... We are turning into shadows. To feel this Clara, with each breath, with the fire of each orgasm, even when the eyes of the living are closing and when we climax climax...

I dictate. She looks at me... Then throws herself into it, her eyes empty. Clara is discreet. She cracks her heart open then – slams it shut.

Night invades the room... time to go to bed... She climbs onto her bed like one descends into a dark well. She gets on like one gets on a nightmare boat. She gets on with her eyes closed.

Full. Stretched out on the bed, watchful… She looks at a flea on the wall. She touches it. Makes it move. I see her in her little room. I see her writing. All alone. I see her as a little girl.

---I will never be old---That – never---Forty and that's it.

I see her old. Quite old quite bitter quite alone. Life never misses the mark. It scythes at the roots. It puts its own full stop at its own time. Life… it's us, yes, us. All. And every one is scared.

Paris. During the quiet hours – we look at each other. This city is a man. Paris is a tired man.

Clara is sleeping and it makes me feel calm. The simple presence of a sleeping someone…

I go out on the terrace and I look at it slowly. The city… The ring-road the ads Sony Hitachi Philips – big letters red or blue. The cars that move quietly on the ring-road. Parc de la Villette. The city afar. Very far… Above the cosmic lights. No stars… not a single star. And this city down there. An immense ditch full of fireflies… And the fishing net is empty. The city… The black waters are shining. You can't escape. You can't open the windows and – the ocean. To see it coming closer, nocturnal. Here, in Paris, to see the ocean like a dead person sees immense things behind a curtain.

Clara… She envies me. "You know… even the simple thought that you there in your room you could die or I don't know… fall sick… nobody knows where you are. Nobody. Nobody could come and see you like this… unannounced… nobody. The door code then you need a key to your hallway. Hidden up there. Nobody to save you. If I had a room like this…"

I see her alone in her room, rue Cadet. I always see her alone. I can't imagine her with someone else. I can't.

Always alone you. Motionless. I see you – writing. Leaning… The city is breathing quietly. No sirens no screams. Evening… And you writing writing… It's been a while already. It's almost night time. Your profile outlined in the twilight. The black lock of hair. Enchanted… That fierce profile. Quietly fierce. The profile of a mask.

And there… A star. In the orange sky of Paris. Another one… Two… The constellation of your life. Your lips – I see your lips move. Help me… Little star. Little sky help me… Change my life. Let it change. Change… Something… Time. The blow of time suspended and. Beauty…

Nobody believes her. Nobody. Yes, I talk about her escapes. To a life full of life, to a life all new. Nobody. She's been saying it for ages – I'm leaving and – everybody chuckles. To Argentina to Morocco I'm going to Morocco! But nothing to do. No one believes her. She wants to leave. Life… I want to stuff her into any plane and – that's it. Let's end your Holy Week. At last! Let's get to the Passion. I feel sorry for her. To get her dead drunk and then – taxi to Charles-de-Gaulle. To carry her in my arms… All the way to the plane. Let her wake up in Polynesia! In the middle of the Ocean. That she loves so much…
She wants to undress from her life. But she stays.

Canada… Madagascar! She reels… She gabs and stays. One day she'll kill herself to change her life. She'll kill herself – like writing a letter. She'll jump from her place – it will be like taking a plane. She'll make phone calls all around and all around she will say she's leaving. At last! And all around they will chuckle. Yes as usual. And then… She'll at last take a plane. From her place. From her 8th floor. One day.

Do you remember, Clara? That nice crazy woman… She thought we were brother and sister you and I. She told us – You both have blue eyes. Blue… All those who have blue eyes are brothers and sisters.

She was so discreet and then her end so atrocious… They still have goose-bumps from it in our hutch. Fire… She killed herself on a low heat. Lying day and night in her room. Day and night… Motionless and alone. Childless. Neighbours' voices. Remote… She wasn't eating wasn't drinking. No screams no words. She peed a little in her bed and then – it was over. Over, Clara… Can you imagine?

You say you will never be old… You used to buy bread for her when you were coming to my beehive. She told you about a child screaming in her head. I didn't see her for a week or maybe two and one day – I come back from your place. Yes in the morning… Very early… Doors open… Firemen… A catastrophe. It's the Dealer who saw her, it was him who called the fire brigade. She wasn't dead yet… It was later… in the hospital… It was there that everything ended. But before she had been alive. In the fire… In the fire around her. I think about it… How. How she did it. They found carbonised newspapers. Bits floating in the air of the room… I think of that night. How…

You don't kill yourself to die, no. No. You don't want to kill yourself, you don't want to go. You kill the world that has gone mad. And you die.

One day she lay down. Lay down for good. And then days nights went by… Her bed – in the middle of a pile of old newspapers. Little by little with her tortoise paw she piles them up in her bed. Around… Paper drifts… She made paper mountains. And then – she set them on fire. She took a lighter and – she set them on fire. It was me yes, me who gave her that dark blue Cricket. It was with that. The lighter – I saw it since then. Ibrahim picked it up. It survived. There was a name scratched on it… It was me, my hand. It had been in my pocket since Russia.

Hell…

You ask me – why… You talk to me and you cry Clara. You ask me why I am trafficking… Women and all… For a precise reason – I reply. I bind people. Women with men. I bind them… Face to face… Here's a dance. That Belgian guy and Natasha. And others…

I needed a room Clara. I will still need it. Always. For me and for Bearcub. A more or less permanent place, a closet, a garret… to finish my thing and – I will shut up then. I don't ask for anything. I can live with nothing. Oat flakes and that's all. Like a workhorse. Like an ass… Oat flakes until I start neighing. I would even stop smoking… it's costly. I would stop everything. Coffee – only standing at the bar. Never on the terrace never again – sitting. And then – I would snuff it… but afterwards. In the end I would be someone else, yes, but afterwards, not right now! You talk about changing Clara. A real change… you want me to change. Alright, but afterwards. Somebody has to die, yes, for it to change somebody has to die. That – yes, that's a change. But not right now, it's for the days to come, for the old days. Right now I need a cranny to finish it, to wrap it up… And then I'll tidy up after myself.

A hidden place I'm looking for. I'm a pregnant beast, a pregnant guy, heavy with life, selfish like four. I'm looking for a place to give birth.
You say – too much night. You say I'm pregnant with night. Alright. Alright. Then my night will give birth to black light.

You say I'm weird. Sick. Maybe, Clara. So be it. When you are sick that's one thing. But when you don't remember what health is anymore – that's a different one altogether.

Gouk is Belgian. Gouk is tall. He fucks a blonde and he writes a mystical book. A Russian girl – it's mystical enough already. A blonde Russian girl is double mystical. Fucking a Russo-blonde… I don't know how he manages Gouk. And then he's writing his mystical book. What might. I almost envy him.

He's slow and canny like a giant panda. He's roaming there. Somewhere.
It's him who lent me this room. For me and Bearcub. Before he had been lying down on a blonde, in this service room. I should say maid's room – given all those mystiqueries… They had been mystiquing quietly cheek to cheek and then the girl fulfilled her role. Effectively. And now it's mine. It's me who lies down here.
Without redheads or blondes I write here. It won't be mystical at all. My business for the time being… I've sewn up the fish mouth. Otherwise Gouk would be back.

And lodging a guy who's about to be sued as a paedophile… That's me talking. Makes you lose your hard-on, doesn't it Gouk? But don't you worry I keep quiet. I don't fuck, and even if – one would have to re-fuck after me, so it's not worth it. I don't take drugs. I don't ask for anything.

Not for MI or any benefits. I'm not old not young not disabled. No right to anything I don't ask for anything, anyone. Nothing at all. I try to exist less than a stray cat. And all the more, Gouk – I'm not writing a mystical book. Who am I? Nobody. Just saying… Aside.

Let them fuck again I say. Again, and more and more! A Cyclops in love. Polyphemus. Natasha! Let him crush your cherry every day and twice or thrice. I beg you the God of Blondes! Spare her… Natasha, be blessed. Your goddess' legs. Your steppe pussy. Fur et cetera… Let it become a lair for that Gouk panda. Let him sleep there enfurred… Bless your heart! The arse of your heart. Amen.

The blonde. Here's the thing with blondes. Guys see a blonde in a blonde for about an hour. Two – max. And then… Then they don't see a blonde anymore. I say this to Natasha – he must see the blonde in you every time. You must be a blonde every day.

Also… His clock must show noon. Always. I'm not a pimp Natasha. I need that bloody room is all. If I were a blonde, me… But I'm not and you – you are. Come on! The Red Army Choir is with you. Let's sing softly Hurray and – go Natasha! He loves Russian songs? I will give them to him. He can't get enough of our barbaric sorrow? I will turn his noon into evening. Yes. Just for him. Yes. He'll get his sorrow dance. Yes – just for him. I'll barbarise him a bit. Local Gouks like getting barbarised. He loves the twilight of the heart? My balls are full of it.

Lovemaking like fox-hunting? You've copped it Natasha… I had warned you about that madman, but you wanted a husband, no matter the price. Well well, didn't you have some loathsome blokes. A mad chatelain. A hunter… You didn't like it at all. Blood on the seats of the 4x4.

A night in the fields… Gunshots everywhere! Bang! Bang! The demonic hunt! Frightened boar, blinded by his Rover. And then their carcasses on the back seat… You didn't like it… And you moaning wiggling under his belly. A crushed doe. He fucked you on the back seat, amid the boars' hard carcasses. You didn't like it at all. So…
You say I'm dirty. DIRTY. Me. Sick, me, a pervert – you say and you hate me. I know it and I know why, yes. I saw you crawling at their feet. Gouk and then that mad hunter. I saw it and you hate my guts. And there you go you are glued, you and Gouk, face to face, with the hatred, with that glue that is the sweat of hatred. Lovers on my back and I carry you, okay but it comes at a price. You two must pay. You whispered words to him about me, not everything, just enough for him to hate me too and to stick more and more to your thighs. Yes. Alright, and then what? Who will be your next enemy?
He's so supportive Gouk, fervently ready for anything as long as you blow his giant dwarf's pecker, it's you who told me, and now you hate me to death! He thinks he loves you, ha, he thinks you love him. It's absorbing, it's all-consuming, emotions like that, and it comes at a price here, a high price.
From boredom, it's a lot better as a remedy, and it's also outlandish, it makes you travel, the blondes, the snow, the Russian soul, all that, it's serious stuff, Gouk, it moves your heart without having to move your arse and this – it has a price here, yes. A whore costs nothing Gouk, a wife – more, but the two of you it's a wonder. You two have an Enemy. A common one. And an enemy, it costs a pretty penny.

And now you my beautiful Slav. You go down too quickly Natasha. And you… You aren't sick, are you?

Your son for whom you keep opening them. He's sick you say, yes, sick, it costs money to be dying, everywhere it costs. You… You aren't mad, are you? All of us… All of us are sick. We hammer away… We run on the ceiling. We sell and resell ourselves. For nothing, really for nothing, we suffer to avoid suffering. We throw our skin, yes, little bit by little bit, into the fire and then there's smoke and it stings and we want to turn our mugs away from it.

Now – let's talk quietly Natasha. Your son will die, Gouk will dump you. You will go to Russia, go home, to your graves, to Novgorod. You will learn how to cut hair, you will get married, you will live a long life with your man and you will tell him about Paris, about France, he will truly love you Natasha, that quiet man, with your hair turned white, with those Russian autumn flowers, frail flowers laid on your son's grave.

Here – I can talk in my sleep and nobody would hear me. I can rave at full blast. All I want… No ceiling no walls…

Our hutch… Avenue de la République. At the back… Yes, right at the back. A dead angle. Written in the hall – GUERILLA IS THE BEST FUCK OF THE REST. In English. And then the smell. Our calling card. They've forgotten to bury someone. No mistake – welcome to our place.

All the dust of the world, all the sadness… Served to us with a soup spoon, a ladle. Turned into shadows. Sad shadows hysterical shadows. Shadows without magic… Maybe this is death. So slow… All those people… Like a spirit

I'm here, a calm spirit. Maybe I'm already dead. It's been a while, who knows?

The neighbour, the old woman, beats her man. A nuclear war is a prettier sight. I see her sitting in that bar across the road. Motionless. She knows that she's dead. Rooted into the ground by the four legs of her chair. The oblivion tower. A fat tower of oblivion. Sad fat – she stuffs herself to feel alive.

---Hellcat! You want to kill me!---her man screams---But before---I will kill you, I will---

Yes – I say – she wants to kill you, yes, she's dreaming of it, yes, she wants to kill herself too.

---Bitch you're so strong! He goes on. He's almost crying---When is this going to end!---Drop dead!

---Me?---Blabbermouth! she retorts---Wank off your nose ---Sissy!---Fuck you! Go fuck your mother!---She won't be disappointed that whore!---When is this going to end---

No, it won't end. It will never end. It will go on… And on… Until there's a dead body. Until one of you kicks the bucket. And beyond… From one life to another, from one flat to another – you'll find each other. To eat each other up. To tear each other to shreds. To chop each other with an axe…

Twilight crawls to my feet. I can't move anymore. I listen to this music. It's been a year – I live here and I won't move. I could die and nobody would know, you have to know the code, yes, to come here. Clara, Gouk, Natasha… The others… They can't follow me here. The angel of death will do the outgoing inventory of fixtures. Maybe he'll come over with other dead. Local souls. They would be wary first, yes, to accept me… And then it'll be alright.

I stay, but why do I stay here? What harvest do you come here for? And what sorrows have you come to forage… A thief in this beehive. You and all the other badly sown seeds… Let the seed die. Let's go into the dark. To stop seeing. Seeing all this. Stop.

You don't move from here. You wait for what will follow. All that slander, all those battle scenes… Cries. Screams.

The guy who calls me "brother"… Ibrahim-the-dealer… he says to me – brother. It made me sick at the beginning but you get used to vomiting within. Every week he goes to the post office. Every week at the post office he goes to the Western Union counter. He sends money to his mother. Every week. He has become Friday. Before God says At ease! – my dealer is there. Planted at the threshold of the post office. A walking tree. He grumbles. It's the only thread that ties him to the cruel stepmother France.

On the weekends he stays home. No girlfriend no boyfriend. His mother and him – that's the whole clan. His brother it's me. If one needs a brother he says – brother. He's a champion this guy. The oldest dealer in Île-de-France.

"Maybe… I should buy… I don't know… A pet. A dog. An animal… A cat. It takes your mind off things. It stops you from letting yourself go completely."

He talks to me talks… He sits down on my ears. Sighs… He says to me – brother. I am only another crazy Ruski for him, one more, but he needs to say "brother", really does, that's the thing. Brother brother brother… My arse. We are just two starving worms gobbling up the dead flesh of that old bitch Europe. Worms that wiggle in the rotting wounds. Roundworms that just eat, shit and eat their own shit again. Brother brother… Worms don't have siblings. For the time being we keep wiggling but the one who will come… The master, yes, the master of that old bitch Europe or simply someone who'd have even a thimbleful of pity for her. He'll exterminate us. Will clean her wounds with a knife, yes, a white-hot knife. He won't put on gloves, him. In one hour. In two hours it will be over. Sing or don't, scream or hide in the dust on the ankles of Allah – the day will come…

Twice he said to me "do the spotting brother. I work alone… Right?" So – I did the spotting twice.

Sometimes he masturbates. The best neighbour – it's the one who makes noise at the same time as you do. It's a dream neighbour. He doesn't try to hide anymore. He leaves the telly on and wanks off in the blue… In the dark… it's so sad… He masturbates and then he comes. Comes laughing. Once I saw his shoulders shudder. He turns his back to me. He drops his head into his hands and he cries… Cries.

He meets women online. He finds them on dating sites. From a café he writes to them. "Don't tell anybody, brother. I am supposed to despise the Negresses. The Arabs despise them. They are 'Abd for us… Slaves but I talk to them. I talk to them about God. To oil the path. It warms up their napes. I listen to them. Those daughters of Africa. From the Congo… From far away. From Zaire… They have booths there, in their countries, specially to exhibit themselves. They all want to leave Africa. To escape… They get sick of my talking about God. They are fed up with it after a while, they say – look, a good dick – this is what you need – for the goddesses to love you! If you want I can show you… To you. Only to you… In the booth…

There're some who are beautiful. They want to come here. Here… For a handful of bills they would do anything for you. For one bill… To come here. To come! By any means. By boat. By plane. By swimming… On foot… On the waters of the ocean. From the black to the blue. They say – I want to come to France. I want to start a real family. With you. There… If only they knew. But they want it! To come here. They can't wait, the chicks… I don't tell them I'm an Arab. I tell them – come, but not a word about being an Arab. A Negress wouldn't come for an Arab. For a white twat, even an old white twat on a minimum pension – yes, but not for an Arab.

I listen to all this. The heart of life is beating. Beating… I don't know much. All this suffering. These people…

I think of my death. I don't want it to be slow. In a dream. But people say you have to deserve it. As if they knew Death. All of us. We are just barely born.

My life… So many rooms, ceilings. Of all those women I have only ceilings left. Windows… It always ended by the window. My back to the dweller – I was looking into the distance. In truth I didn't know all those who had been sleeping with me, giving me money… Who said – they loved me… Who hated me in the end. Who had been saying to me – a child. Who had been saying to me – love… So many faces… So many words. So much heat. Fire. Ceilings.

Here – I'm far from my land. Very far. I think of the downstairs neighbour, the fat one. She lives three metres below my feet but we are farther from each other than the stars. Light years apart…

I hear her screams… "Job? I've knocked about! A tyre I am… Flat. Knackered! Knackered… Let the living work! Let the whores toil! Freedom to the dead! Work – it's for the living."

A child on the second floor cries. Mummy! Mummy! Don't go! I'm scared! I don't want to… leave the light on! I'm scared… mummy! I did a poo…

She leaves. The door slams. The crying less loud… Faint. Then silence.
I welcome the evening. Like a spirit… A dazed spirit I listen to this life. I savour it. Cry by cry blow by blow drop by drop – I take in everything. Like the soil of the steppe takes in the rain. I soak up everything and I become heavy. Very heavy. Heavier than the world. I can go down low, very low. Where there's nothing. Nothing. No screams no cries.

The oldie's dogs are barking. Another oldie. On the ground floor. They almost miaow. It's weird. Maybe she's dead… I haven't seen her in a while. She's been slow and sick. So bent she could only look at the ground. She said once – I have a toad on my heart… And now – maybe it's over. No one to open the door. No one to cry. Only her dogs cry. Only animals cry over us.

The dogs call… Animals' souls. The reinforcement. They will come. She loved them so much… Yes. They will come their souls. They will touch her with their noses… Her hands… Her face. Gently silently they will guide her soul.

The girl from the third floor is talking… Talking… She's going to get fucked to the core. She's going to open them. Shortly. She's laughing… Then the silence of a kiss as thick as her arse.

This girl – she's our Callas. She gets fucked by an angel. For a girl to sing in orgasm… But Clara is doubtful. Fifty fifty. She thinks La Callas is faking. A woman knows how to flush out another woman. She lies La Callas! But never mind, she sings for us. For the whole courtyard. Our diva.

To love the dead is one thing. Not to despise the living – is another one altogether.

Into the distance… Yes, I want to look into the distance. My eyes… let them rest. And see… Only to see. I would like to be eyes only. Only eyes with no heart no hands no mouth. To be only eyes. To see everything and feel nothing. To become eyes. The oldest eyes in the world.

When you touch its true wounds – it becomes hostile, the world. But why so much wrong… So much sadness… You put your fingers into its true wounds and – it grows enraged. It grows enraged the world. Grows hostile.

Don't touch it anymore, don't touch anything here. Leave it… Be the eyes. Only the eyes.

Fear. Yes – you see fear… All of us we fear all the others. Even yes, even those we love most – fear us.
My life… What a dream. I have to see someone who can read the signs, who can plunge his hands into omens, who can sew wounds in the dark. I want to find him. Talk to him. Let him answer me, yes, let him tell me everything in one word.

To say one word. To whisper it. To whisper it so softly… Only one word. One. It could save. It could save everything. But what if it doesn't save… And if I'm only a poor monster? A child with no magic and it's over, the party… Then – I am sick.

My wife will tell them. I see her saying – he is sick. The poor bastard…

Me – sick. My words are sick… My brain. My heart is sick. Its beat, too. Here is the dance… The end. Maybe not. I stay here. Yes to me. Yes to this. I don't move from here anymore. Things will come. People – I don't need the living anymore. Not you not your stories, it's over. I know it – we'll all meet again. We'll be reborn again… It will never end. Again and again… And – we'll die. All. And

I – I stay here… My life. Yes to you. I'm telling you – yes. I'm staying.

To find the pitch of your life. The right pitch. Not even its sense, no… Its pitch. Your father, your mother… Babania. People you saw only once… In the trains in the railway stations in the streets. So many faces… Eyes… Eyes. The eyes of those who are dead. The life of the living. Clara… Gabriel… Damiana. Those who are at a whisper's distance. At a cry's… Those who are being born… At this precise moment. Now… Those who take their first breath and. Those who breathe their last… The pitch. A small thing… The right pitch. No dialogue. We communicate too much. Too much. Yes, all is said. That's all there is.

A hospital for oldies. At Le Mans, opposite – I had the jail. Here – the hospital. Nothing but old women at the end of their tether. Not a man. Not one. As if there had never been any men on earth. Men die before that. They escape their fate, men. And women, they go on little sip by little sip. In the end only old women with pets are left. I watch these old women. They talk. They are in the distance. I see their mouths opening.

I watch them every morning. I see their empty beds. Then the next the new ones arrive. I watch them talk. Their mouths… Mouths of fish gasping for breath.

Women women a crowd of women… Never a man. And you Dim what are you doing here… You? A man. People leave… All gone. Men women. You see – they are going. You see… That agony of old women behind the glass. Death of a man. The fall of one hair. A long long fall of a single hair…

Rooms… All those rooms there. The nurses tired smiling exhausted. Making the beds. They are white. Benches covered in snow… Dragging bodies from one room to another. Turning over, washing and turning back. I see it well from here. So clearly… That oldie, her bird's shoulders hunched. Frightened she is. And the girl, the nurse's leaning over. She's grimacing. She's screaming… She's going to hit her. That old woman… Maybe. There are some who do. Hit. I've seen it from here.

I watch watch… All of it enters me and I become the eyes.

It never ends, this. Never. Even the light gets tired, yes even the light wears off from flying towards us. Even stars die… Their light can't take it anymore.

To fall silent for good. Very quietly to be silent without screaming. I saw men falling silent for good. Leave it as it is. Leave it all here don't touch anything anymore. Take your soul into your mouth. Don't touch it anymore.

Water running in the loo. Splishhh splishhh splishhh. You would think it's whispering. It keeps me company in the evenings.

I lie down. It's night. No lamp. No, I don't turn on anything. It's my black light… I see everything. In that black light like in a sarcophagus – I wait.

It's just up the road from the Père-Lachaise my room. Mostly alone – I don't suffer anymore from the light of dusk. That light doesn't make me moan anymore. I watch the passers-by, Chinese people, Chinese women with bandy legs, old Black guys with pink shirts. I watch the White. Most of them are grey. Grey… I see old men who waver. Their chicks smell DOSH. They pick up the scent of fear. The big funk… It's Love – I translate. Liuboff. Bless you the arse of youth. The old farts, slobbery, hearts muzzled, are so nice. So squashed… As soon as one had a heart attack – no more fucking… Crawling. In fear. The fear of emptying their balls once and for all. To croak on top of his old woman – ah no. So one daydreams then. With a young one. Balls in the pockets, yes, you have to be reasonable. To come under anaesthetic. The true old age is when one is happy, but happy to climax without croaking. To empty your balls and find yourself still alive, here's the thing, the rest of it – to hell. The old guys they know the thing. Desire has no wings. True desire, it crawls.

The man smells of the sea when he pulls out of a woman. Melancholy.

I remember in Sebastopol I saw a couple of sailors they walked arm in arm. The boulevard was empty, the boulevard was white like a bone in the steppe. It was the South.

I knew a guy who fucked corpses. He told me he loved them… He told me he couldn't stand the living. Never could. The dead aren't jealous – he used to say.

I knew another one. He was a plumber. He loved sniffing dirty underwear. In his customers' homes. He was saying mmm I plunge my head into the dirty laundry basket and I sniff… He was very nice. Two kids and a wife…

Sometimes there are things. It isn't so dead here. Two girls, two friends are walking by. High-heeled girls. Clip clop… They're walking by like a horse. You'd say a mare in our courtyard. I see them with my ears. Their buttocks are moving. Kitchen sounds, smells… It's coming from down below, it smells good. It smells of life.

La Callas is sleeping, deeply shagged she's sleeping. She screams and then when it's all over – she falls asleep. Her spirit leaves, yes, her spirit must leave after a shag so long. So intolerably good.
I can see her from my room. She sings she sopranises our yard. Her heart she puts her heart into it.

It's the opera of the poor. Carmen of the poor. For all those who are jobless here… For all those who are half-dead. The people of our yard – she sings for us.
I say to myself who can sing alone? Us here… Who's able to sing alone. Who? How sad all of this. Who would sing the real life for us – alone. We're only able to touch ourselves in silence… In such crowded silence, fuck it.
Let us all croak here. All. Kalashnikoved to death.

The world… The old. No sign of change, no clue. Nothing. Everything like before. Guys pissing standing, gals pissing crouching. Nothing then.
The martyrs of the City? The little people? There's no more little people. Those who suffer here… It's biomass. It's run-down kitchen garden. The little people, they have been invented. To grab their souls. To fatten them and then – grab.
There're no more little brothers… Who'd want to be your brother, Dim? Only that old guy. That dealer. They should be reinvented the little people. They should be reinvented the brothers. There aren't enough of them for everybody – the little people. They should be protected. What is it, their name? Their name is nobody. So… Each generation reinvents its little people and then – betrays them.
Each generation builds slums and breathes souls into them. To populate holes with little souls… To betray them later on.

You say… My violent tenderness and all. Alright. But to ape the poor… When that guy, a pal of Gouk's came over, that so-called fucking publisher… Wearing a coat with holes in it, him, filthy rich, rich to the point of numbness, in a holey coat! What contempt but what disdain, ape! Playing poor! Live it! Live their nights. Their rooms with their smells their dead. You, die with them. Die there where their old men die, their old women who don't even speak French. Who don't speak at all. Who fall silent and live like that. Go, ape them to the max! Let it fly. Ape the hanged. Clutch their feet. That's no joke. Live their days. You. Die with them. In the same rooms. Climb into their beds. Lie down there and die instead of them. Them, the poor… they die unknown, them. When they die no one even knows they had ever lived. They will always be poor. Ad infinitum. From one life to another. From one death to another.

But him he's looting. And so I beg Death of the Poor to come for him. For him, especially, let Death come, let her leave her kingdom, she won't be disappointed. Let Death nail his tongue to the ground. Death, don't let him out for a pee. Dress him into clothes from the corpses of the poor.

But calm down… Shhh… Think of yourself. Who would come, who would close your eyes. You should eat a little. Come out of this room. Yes – go out… Look at the bats. There… So lovely. Gone hunting. What a flight… Look. Look. How they fly… Fragile. These skylarks of the dusk... Blind souls. Go out… Come out of this well. Go up.

In Paris it happens to me – in the evenings… Evenings force me out. The street attracts me. It attracts all

the loners. It holds a strange power over the loners. I run down the stairs.
I look at people who look at the clothes shops, I look at those who eat on the footpaths. The weather is good, yes it's a nice evening. They kiss each other, stroke each other, because the weather is lovely, yes it's a nice evening. They laugh chat but why are their eyes so sad. Where does it come from? They eat they drink. Where from?
Their hands are sad, hands that stroke why are they sad? So nervous. I imagine those who didn't come out. All those who are at home at this moment. Who cry eat fuck kiss masturbate fling moans at each other, who breathe loudly and more and more and stifle the sperm…
I think of all those who are dying in this city. At home, in the hospitals… All those who are dying terribly scared. Those who leave into that fear. Those who die without noticing and who even dead are scared. Those who are leaving their remains at this moment. I think of those who kill themselves. They succeed and they are afraid to succeed – and it's too late. Too late. I see the walls of this city. The warm stones tonight. Stones hold some warmth tonight… An old warmth. Don't get excited Dim. All the loners have bastard eyes. Don't get euphoric… Keep walking… Keep walking. And all of that enters me. Like a Babylon whore a tired whore I cross the city – I'm heavy… pregnant with these stones.

The narrow streets. Lilac evenings are so slow. You hear in the distance – whirr… A car. It goes by and – silence. Chirp chirp swifts are whistling above Notre-Dame-du-Travail. And the smell of hot rails, the smell of tired iron.

It isn't the solitude of the soul, no. No. It's my body, my body that is lonely. And I can feel love through the

walls… Like a Babylon whore in glory and in tears I walk by. Like a whore who greases her body with human fat, oils herself with human fat and dances. A whore who wants to touch someone. To find a body… To touch it. Not stones. Not these old stones. A body… In this city in vapours of piss I walk from stone to stone. Under the ground. On the surface. From one mountain of stones to another… Buildings… Walls warm from loving. Stones I can squeeze in my hands and centuries of love cries would drip from them. Whispers that beget us – give birth to us. Chimneys up high and. So quick the sky… We go up in smoke. We burn, my god – we burn… Our bones. Our nails. Skins of our loves under our nails. The heat of whispers rises above this city. In smoke we rise.
A whore cries in me. Hot are her tears. No rage, no… the old whore in me, she knows how one ages in one go. In one go – one puts on two thousand years, my soul, it knows that. Getting old in the fire. Getting old all your life on a low heat. Go up in smoke. Rise from here.

In this city I walk looking for a body. I speak to no one. I phone no one to say that I'm alone. That my soul is dancing and… That's what I say to no one. A whore with a dancing soul I walk by. I calm down yes. Coming back in the room I will smell bodies loving each other and I will calm down. I will look at the roofs. Slowly I will see brooks of smoke in the sky. Hundreds of smokes and mine. Mine. Too much fire. Too much… It's so slow. My whore will close her eyes and. I will be very quiet.

I say – a man needs a woman and a window. A woman can't be the window for a man. She lives indoors. She looks at the man who looks into the distance. Me, I have only one window. I am only a window. There is something prophetic in my life. In any life... All you need is a bit of a break. To catch your breath a bit. To pick up the remains of your life in your fist. And the forgotten words will come back. Ancient words. They call them ill words... They will come the old words. They will scare us. They will heal us. It will hurt it will make creases in our skin so that the real thing could hide in them. My life, I will see it naked. With no adjectives. Fear yes, fear is in the creases. Fear is the only real thing, my friend.

My eyes... I WANT TO SEE NOTHING! NOTHING! Only mountains. Mountains alone. High mountains snowy mountains. It will do me good. No caves no grottos no abysses no ocean no sea either. Mountains highly white – they are alone and I am alone. There... To look into the distance far into the distance. No more holidays by the sea. No more fucking beaches. Those whore hothouses. Die! All of you! Let us all die! Oh no, no more beaches or girls... Adventures... Oh, that... Those Olympic Games... No. I'm fed up with it... Mountains... I want the mountains. To think of it. Everywhere in the city I will think of mountains. Everywhere. In the streets in the cellars in the metro and on the bus. From the basements to the garrets. From the street market to the supermarket... Everywhere. And of nothing else! Not of my soul... My soul is an old air hostess. To close my eyes... To think of nothing. Not girls not beaches. Only mountains... High mounts. And then – to close my eyes. And then – to sleep sleep, and they would be there.

Like a rich man. Yes, I live like a rich man. I eat little. It's the same – I'm continuing. I wear holey jeans.

Like a rich man. They have taken it all from the poor. Even the holes. Their music. Their dance. Their tattoos.

The Zulu. They don't even know the fire but – they wear new jeans. Let them have the fire. Let them learn how to use. Let the forests party! Let the jungle blow up. Let the Zulu have fun.

Like your mother you're going to adopt war fashions. A survival system. You have to become old. To live like you're old. Two pairs of shoes. One jacket. A warm jacket against dampness. A jumper. A pair of gloves and your scarf.

And then – more. You will push it even more. Another hole in the belt… What are you going to eat?

I asked no one for anything. I regret nothing at all. Over. Soon Dim soon – everything will be over. You will become a spirit, a calm spirit and you will need nothing. Nothing at all. Like a fish needs an umbrella. Soon Dim – it will be the punchline of the story. Life will put the full stop. No more juice in its pen, it's scratching already. And then – it's past noon, the flowers clam up. Soon.

If you're poor you have to learn some little things. A poor must be light. Light… To make do with very little. You must be alone. Yes, that – it's the most important part if you're poor. To know how to retreat. Like an old dog. Like Friend. To be gifted for misery… We're finished if we're too gifted.

In the evening I don't cook. A bowl of rice yesterday. A bowl of white rice, Himalayan snow white. To look high up! Finally – you must become old. An old Chinese man. An old Chinese a thousand years old… To become the cat of the old Chinese man and to eat after him. To make do with his leftovers. To squint and to see the mountains.

True misery has no autumn no winter, it never passes. You must be light yes. All is there. All. This lightness is the heaven of the poor. This lightness. I'm affected by it. Almost. But that… I can't be an old Chinese man, no I can't.

There's no mystery. If there's one – it's the lightness of loving and dying. If you're poor you have to be ready to love and die anywhere. To love? To love, it's for the others. To love…
But to croak, that – yes. Anywhere. With little help. Without. In an ambulance. With or without anaesthetic. With people around. With no one. There's no mystery.

Where is it your global warming? Let me hold another few days… A week. Hold on. Your son… She'll take him back his mother and you could let it go. To resume going down. But for now – hold on! You aren't alone Dim. Bearcub… But it's cold… Now… Your tights Clara! Your tights you leave them lying around. Everywhere… Like a snake you never put your old skin back on, Clara. Where are they? I have to find them. I'm cold Clara…
Usually they turn up by themselves. Under the mattress, between books… From anywhere. They still keep your warmth… Yes Clara that's what I am like. They keep your warmth… It's magic that snakeskin. Let them turn up! I'm going to put them on. Under the jeans. The most lightly dressed girls – are never cold… Never… the most naked – never cold. A secret… What's their heating? Tell me Clara. What's happening, why am I so cold. It's freezing Clara. Tell me. Tell me the heat Clara. Tell me how hot it is in your place. Tell me what heat is.

We haven't seen each other for centuries, quite a few centuries. We did say call you later, yes, and it was over, all over. We haven't seen each other since. We won't see each other here again. You will go back home, to your land, to the Atlantic, to Rochefort. You will love a man, a good man, a kind man made of one piece, with no potholes or cracks. You will be happy Clara, really, you will want a child with him and you will get pregnant, yes, you will carry in you a boy. Life will become so tangible, so true… One day the doctor will tell you – sorry, Madam, but your baby is ill. He will talk talk, that you have to think about it to take your time and see, to weigh everything, yes to weigh it well and – to come back to see him quickly.
You and your man – the two of you before the ocean so calm – everything weighed in silence, everything said, you are going to keep your son. He will be born on New Year's Eve. Motionless for life he will be between you, and life will become even more real even more, more and more naked. You will be before the ocean the three of you, calm, tired, very tired. He'll push the wheelchair – to bring the kid home to bed and you will stay alone. At the moment, yes, right at the moment of your breaking down in tears you will feel a fatigue, a strange fatigue that is the bastard daughter of grace.

It was an apparition. I wasn't drunk. Delicately awaken like St Peter in the prison of King Herod. With a punch from the Angel who came to rescue him.

It's him. Him… The Angel of the North. Come from far away to kill me. The Angel of the North with a shaved head... Sent by whom – this I don't know. By whom… But I will know soon. And now he's roaming around, son. He's roaming waiting for the right moment. Now... Listen to me, son. On purpose. Sent on purpose. Come on purpose to kill me. An angel, it doesn't hang around – come on purpose, yes, not to air his balls! Sent specially to get my skin. Literally. To skin me. Alive, dead – no matter. Come from far away specially to get my skin. Sent for this purpose. Resolutely. Mark my words, son.

You see... Each angel has his own mission. You don't see them hanging around the city. They don't hang around. No, they don't turn up for nothing. If an angel pulls it out – it strikes. If an angel comes – it's for sure. They don't make mistakes. An angel comes to make an announcement. To break your shadow in half. In full sun – in half. To measure his share. And – to push your innards aside.

I saw him for the first time at the Paris Book Fair. He turned up – tall. To ask me to sign his copy. To write something. Whatever.

He was smiling. Smiling... And his finger – it was stroking my mugshot on the back cover. That – I got the message. His finger was closing my eyes... That movement, yes, I know it well. Closing the eyes of a dead person. Mine. Smiling...

---To whom?--- The name, yes I wanted to hear his name. All. All angels errant spirits ghosts evil revenants – they each have a name, son. But there... There's a moment to ask for their name. You must ask them – the name! It's very very important, son. Vital.

"To the one who comes from far away..." He was pronouncing it slowly. As if dictating. For me to catch it. No dribbling. Sure. He had no accent. Messengers, they don't stutter, don't lisp, don't sough either.

I – I wanted to know his name. And there – a bad sign, son. Very. If an angel or a spirit doesn't tell you his name. Doesn't want to tell you… It's bad. Really. He must have a name the angel. He must tell you. Where from and who.

I say to him – alright… Alright. That's it then. He's come.

I'm freezing. No heating here. This whorish room will kill me. So be it. And Son… He's sleeping. Like a rock, yes, to make the dead envious.

Move out of here like quicksilver Dim! Quicksilver doesn't freeze. The Ural Mountains! Even to think of it – I freeze. I know what I'm talking about. Two years of Yakutia. You don't get rid of it like this. So much the better. The Laptev brothers' sea. Those two brothers, mysterious like their sea. Two brothers…

Peasants who disappear… It was done on foot at the time. Emigrants from the villages vomited by the cities. Evicted. Lost killers… All sorts of stray searchers. Errant… At the time. Not even on horseback. On foot. On sledge. On dogsled.

Two years of the North Pole. Two years on the shores of the frozen Styx. White as far as the eye can see. Ice… I feel dizzy.

Two years on the shores of the Arctic Ocean. Land army? No. There isn't any – land. Ice army. Tiksi. Lost army. An inch from the Pole. Earth doesn't revolve. We don't grow older. We live like snails. No more Time. Stopped. A day – three months. An insomniac Sun. Then it conks out. A night – the same. Three months. The rest of it – twilight… Full stop. And when you get the hell out of there – it puts a hundred years on you.

Irkutsk. Chita. Far away. You see… And then farther and farther still. Baikal. Angarsk. Hundreds of kilometres of silence. Infinite silence. Silence all around… Everything is infinite there. Silences, efforts…

Come on. It was a race. A race against the cold. Against infinity. Against death. Against life. A struggle… Yes. Not a lightning-fast fight for survival. A long struggle… Against sleep. Against mirages. Against the cold. Body-to-body. Forward. Always forward. All the fights drown in the heat. In blood… It ends. But polar nights – last. Last…
And then the wolves, son. You must never leave the dogs alone. Never. The "grey ones", they don't mess with men so easily. But if… A pack of dogs. A pack bawling with loneliness… Loneliness bigger than the moon. Bigger than the heart of a star… Then – the wolves, those silent spirits – kill. Pick the strongest and – strike. In silence. No growling. Like shadows.

A lead she-dog. My own… I must have one. The lead she-dog. For the road to my country to be bumpless. Beyond abysses… If the angel has come to take me back there. To my country… Cold… Cold. There they still have seasons. Who? Who would it be – my lead she-dog? A she-wolf – that would be the best. Dante, him… He had a lion in his pack. A she-wolf. A panther. He will lend her to me. A starved she-wolf, emaciated from rage. She knew, yes how to go about with the spirits. Spirits in a tizzy. She'll manage. We'll see, son, we'll see. My pine isn't old enough yet. My lashes not heavy. And the curtain that will fall – hasn't been woven yet.

The she-wolf will lead me. Forward. To run by her side. Aha! The pack of shadows… Aha! Aha!

The snow is hard. Aha! The sun is tardy! Cold… Pines are cracking.
They run the shadows, they fly. Invisible by my side. Dogs! No squabbling! The she-wolf is leading you. Their empty eyes darken… Forward. Aha! The cry of the North. Aha!

It's belated tonight. Let's run. Until the night curls up, its nose tucked into its tail – let's run. The blizzard… It stops everything.

A short halt in the night. The race towards dawn. The snow grows old. Hardens. The cold… Let it last, last, let it make the road hard. Easy. The road from one halt to another. A blind road. Man is alone, son.

Children… They feel me. They know me. They can't come and see me – but a child's soul will come. It will come here. And – without closing its eyes… No tears – it – will look.

But this is the hardest… Son. My son. It was in the previous century... I had a family. Bearcub… My little wife. It's over now, now – nothing but memories. Like everything that is hard – it will stay in the present tense.
In a small town I see myself. They're going on holiday Bearcub and his mother. I was watching them leave from my son's bedroom. They are gone. He and his mother. That room, yes, and his empty bed… Son.

They must be far already. They are crossing the mountains of Auvergne. Those old mountains full of iron. Red like a skinned cow.

The fireplace. Wooo… Woosh-woosh it blows in there. There is nobody… And it blows in the chimney. I see myself lulling my son. I sing to him and there's that woosh-woosh in the chimney. That wind. Woosh-woosh… That old chant. So old… So slow. All that…

He falls asleep quickly, my son. With me he falls asleep quickly and… I am all alone. Alone. I think of his death. It's the wind. In the chimney the wind is blowing. Everywhere… Everywhere on earth this wind… And I'm alone. Alone. I listen to this chant.
I think of my death. It calms me. Lulls me… Those lullabies. Those funeral chants. I listen to this chant in the chimney… Woo-oo-oo… I think of his death. He isn't sick, no. But the true lullabies are so close to funeral chants. I don't look at him. To be so close… So close to a soul.
My son. His lashes. His closed eyes. I don't look into his closed eyes. No, not that… I see him so close… His face rounded by sleep. The open moon of this face. And I think of his death. The wind! It whistles whistles its song. It lasts hours and hours. Nights… We become old. So old… And the wind. It sighs the wind… So tired. It sweeps away everything on earth.

My son. The net to catch my soul. When I think of his death. My night heart. My day. My twilight… My moon… You… When you die… I think of your death and. I'm here. With you. Sitting. The wind… It's blowing, the wind. It will blow on and on. But why this anguish… This wind. It isn't from here. I recognise it, this wind. It came for me. For me… don't be scared son. Not for you, no. It is here for me. This wind… Sleep peacefully. Don't listen to this wind… Its chant. Sleep quietly. It has come for me.
It blows the wind in the steppe. Something is coming… Something blind… An old Parca with scissors is in this dark room. Very quiet, very mad. Something is approaching.

Night is howling it wants to come in. It doesn't bother him, not at all. He's sleeping well, son. Not the wind not the night, they don't bother him. Night loves children.

Do you hear them? The geese flying up North. Geese flying in the night… High night. Above Paris their cries are flying… Flying.
In this room, in my Père-Lachaise roost I'm alone. I'm dead at this moment, yes like this, just like I am – lying on my mattress… Listening to the cries of the geese. Far away already the geese are far already and. No one… No one. I just have to reflect on all this – it gives me a strange sort of strength. And my hands. I look at my hands. Who am I?! Who?... The hands of my days are empty. Empty… And the hands of the night have nothing.

And the wind blows in the city. In the orange night sky… Woo-o-o-o blows the wind.
My cells are full of this wind. This breath… The song of a man lulling his son. Life… A whisper in the storm. Life… It's too much imagination, too much. My son my little feather. A drop of milk in the night.
His little postcard. He scribbles for me "I went out on a boat. Not a big boat. A small boat. It is white and it is a bit dirty…"

It wasn't just any boat, no. It wasn't a big boat. A small one. A small white boat and a bit dirty!

He gave me a drawing he had done specially for me. She is furious… This lioness… He drew her specially. For me. So that she'd protect me.

There are dragons. Then a snake. And then – an angel. The angel is weak but he is going to attack the dragon and the snake. It happens at night. There's also the Great Bear… But he comes in the end. In the end.

I keep all this… His drawings hanging on the walls. My talismans. It's evaporating, yes little by little it will crumble. Very slowly it's going away. Pains, things… go away. The rest of it – I still have an angel. A dragon and a bear hanging on the walls. The walls will crumble too. The drawings… And then you will get older. Cave in day after day. Bend your knees. Almost not there anymore… For the final sprint you have to keep some strength, so put some aside. Look at them – your talismans. Look at them every day. Every evening. It will help you to make it through the night.

You will die and everything will vanish. Everything will be forgotten. Everything. You won't recognise this world. Not this room not this city so gentle so woman tonight. You will look everywhere and – nothing. You will recognise nothing at all. Not the beloved faces not your shoes not these drawings. And you will leave for good.

The circle do you see it? Around me. Around the monster… To become an enemy to his son. I am an enemy to my son? No.

We are only blood. The same blood for one and the other. They think that I am a danger to you. That I am mad. Mad… What do they know about the mad… They say – yes, they think that I could do you harm. To you. To my blood. To my little feather. Yes and they want to attend. They want to see it. They want to watch the show. A madman who spreads out his wings. A madness that reaches right into his heart. They say that I could, yes that it's possible that I could want to harm you. That my love is like a sickness. My love is a sickness for you. They write to your mother that this relationship is sickness.

I don't have bad dreams, no. It's been a while since I had. I sleep well now. Before – yes, I was nightmaring myself every night. I un-learnt how to sleep like a sparrow that un-learnt how to walk.

But now – I sleep without dreams.

I tied you. I tied you up well. Yes. I tied you to my back. You were small and I was typing. I was typing gently. The keyboard is soft and you on my back you were sleeping. I was rocking and you were sleeping… I was typing, I was rocking and lulling you. We were together you and I. We were on a swing… On a heart-rocking horse. You were falling asleep quickly. I was singing something, humming. And now they say I'm mad. They are going to take you from me. Your mother has nothing to do with it. She hasn't tasted love. She hasn't cried over two hearts. And I, I have two hearts. Yours and mine. You've drunk love. Yes, you too have two hearts, you just haven't noticed it yet.
Once you asked me and you papa are you going to die and I said yes. We were walking, do you remember, we were walking near the prison. And you asked me again and again… Am I going to die too? I?... I smoked. Then I lit a second one. I said nothing. Nothing. You will live this question. Live. With all that… And you know, your drawings… I keep them on the walls. Your dragon your bear your angel, all. Your red dragon almost brown it protects me from dreams and your bear wrestles gently like a friend with your angel and nobody gets the upper hand.
After me the world will heal over. And everything will be gone. My son… I was talking to him about people I loved.

About my grandmother… My dogs my friends. About my places, about the snow… I'm not from here, yes I'm from another country and I talk to him about the snow. Our games in the cold… Under the falling snow. Everything is timeless, yes timeless. We play. But suddenly it's dusk – and – we're far from home. Far and – the shadows have a colour never seen before.
I tell him the steppe and the wind. Woooo woooo howls the steppe, I show him and we giggle and then we don't giggle anymore.
We see, we see this. The two of us we see. The steppe in summer. The small falcons. The midday sky that sharpens their cries Kew! Kew!

I don't tell him the face of my dead grandmother. No. I don't tell him those red hours before the sunset. I was with her in the room. She was there… But all that is too much. Too much. I say nothing. I don't tell him death not men's not beasts' not birds'.

All that… My son will lose it, yes for sure, on his way and then… Step by step we forget the faces of our dead. Little by little. We don't hurt life anymore. We aren't able to sharpen a knife. A moment comes when we don't injure anymore… Life becomes blunted.

Night… Listen to me. I'm talking to you. Night, give me what is mine. Not your children, not your sorcery. Not your rats buried at the crossroads. Not your dolls with punctured eyes. Not the thick drops of blood in the dust. Not my lost loves' hairs… No. Give me my little fish back. Alive. My son… Alive.
Night, you've everything. Yes. You've all your children. Whores on the markets as your figureheads. They're proph-

esising for their sons. Night – you've everything. Give me my son back. A drop of milk in the night, my son… A swallow's chest. I'm the salt of your blood, son. I'm the vermillion of your blood. The red of your blood I am and the white.

My poor little wife… She hits him. She's exhausted. She says he doesn't sleep anymore Bearcub. Since you left he doesn't sleep a wink. He's sad.

She hits him and she says "oh I love you". She screams, yes and. When she screams – she screams. Céline is a teacher. Teachers they scream loudly and for a long time. She has a steel gullet the teacher. She whines – oh I love you. My little sweet burden… My angel heart!

This is what she says – no kidding – it's the heart speaking "my little sweet burden". What a throat!

Then she hits him again. Screams "oh I love you", "my little sweet burden". And again – a smack. I'm not there. I'm in Paris but. All this… These chants. How infinitely sad all this. How sad.

My poor wife. She only wanted to be sheltered. Yes, she wanted to be sheltered from life. To hide. Simply sheltered that's all.

I say to myself – she takes him for a drum, our son. To love and to beat. Love-beat.

They want to take him, they write me these quivering letters the social workers.

One… Fat and gracious she had a body as white as lard. Whiter than the snow. Her buttocks were doing rub-rub I thought I had a pony in the room. She was pretty though. In "an English girl in heat" kind of way. I was observing her. Quiet in my corner. Those rub-rubs of a little lady… She

said – I have two boys and I would be game for more but my husband isn't ready.
I was in my corner quiet. I didn't do anything. Nothing. I was quietly observing her.
To make babies to her… one would need Dionysus' balls…. But she wasn't worse than others. She had patience.

My wife leaves the room. We are there and we are alone. So alone she and I. I feel her this lady. She doesn't want to stay alone with me. In this room so large. The room of the little one. It's large yes, and now the walls are beginning to move. It becomes small the room. A cell almost.

I see my shadow on the wall. We don't move neither I nor it. My shadow… So detached…

It makes me wistful all this. This woman and I. There are two of us and the two of us are scared.

I know it… This sadness in her eyes. She can do nothing for me and I – nothing for her. I turn away from her. Like two dead people we are. We are dead to each other. Like the dead we turn away from each other.
It isn't love we are craving. Life… It is simply life we are craving. That's the worst.

And then. He started to cry. Without words tears were running. Running… No words no faces no rage. Tears of a child overwhelmed by sorrow. Overwhelmed… And the women? They are embarrassed the women. My future ex, her girlfriend and my future ex mother-in-law. Here's the team. They're always there when there're things to cry over. They make a stand. In front of us. Hankies and all… They're extremely embarrassed. They are hating me cordially. And we… I and my son? We're two strangers here. Total strangers.

I comfort him. From me to him. I whisper… I hum. Nothing to do, he doesn't want I DON'T WANT – you to go. Ten minutes and my train will be gone. Sobs… He's crying louder. Huge sobs. The women are there – they are savouring it. They are drinking his tears. They want it to never end. Let him collapse from sorrow. Let him choke and me with him. They don't want it to end. Oh no… To close their eyes? To put their fingers into their ears? For me to stop existing. They would be happy. Let them rejoice.

They want me – to disappear. To be dead. To be forgotten. And even – to have never existed at all. To be deader than the dead and no cross no fire no name. They feel like they're crucified these women and they are happy. To cause pain, not too much but to do it… To see pain. To see the entire road to pain.

And we, son, we throw ourselves at each other. We crucify ourselves in turns, in a loop, arms spread. Short arms. And the longer ones. We hug each other, no more words, son.

The women are there. Nothing has moved. The women they – are still there. They are there when we are born. They are there when we die. Always there.

They are going to take him. My son… To literally kidnap him. I'm a danger to him. You you're sick. Your words are sick your gestures are sick your silences and your dreams. Even your clothes – your rags – are sick. Your scarf… You've been wearing it since your mother died. Yes. Nothing to say… Your gloves – the same. They also come from her. You're looting your dead.

They are going to take him. They will come, they will dress him, then say – You don't want to kiss your father? Go say goodbye to him.

I… Why am I so calm, I don't cry, don't scream, don't rip my jumper, it would be easy though, my old jumper! Easier than a zip! You're going to take your train. No insults, calmly, slowly, like in a nightmare. You're going to sit down and then you're going to look, for a long while you're going to look through the window. Fold yourself up. The true things are in the folds. Go gently. Come on… Let's keep some venom for later. You, you aren't even retired. You don't even have a car. Don't waste your venom. Keep a little bit of agony for the last supper. We are taught not to cry. From rage, ah that – yes that comes all by itself. Not from sorrow not from sadness not from rough weather of the soul. But from rage – yes.

I'm alone and I walk to the train station. Bang-crash! It's a building site. Only the corridors are open. Everything blocked all around. Trench on the left, yellow soil on the right. Complete detour. My arse! He's a train to catch.
Fog is overwhelming me. I see cranes, machines… Faces go by. Yellowish faces. Go by. It's like a dream all this…
My little wife, hold on. Just – two more years. Then you'll get some relief with another one. You will get married again, to a low-ranking civil servant with his own two kids in tow, constipated of wallet, but it's good, you'd said that – it's good for the couple. Small stocky stubborn thick-headed – he'll love you, marry you, dispense smacks slaps kisses evenly to your team. He'll love skiing, cassoulet, red jackets, you, Son, and his own. And you, you will age well, a little deaf and smiley, in good health, curious of everything, you will die old, amid a cluster of children, grandchildren, great-grand, heavy with oblivion, deaf entirely and happy.

Talk my mother-in-law… Talk. I have to work. I have a wife and a kid to take care of – you say. I must give them their pittance. Yes, talk some more. Further. Yes I know this. Horns in the ground – plough Dim. Talk Madam talk. I'm not so absent Madam… I see myself on the roads. Leading to you.

Small towns in winter. Night. You want to pass through them the quickest possible. Yes. To cross them with your eyes closed. This old car dawdles, it doesn't want, like an old whore it doesn't want to serve anymore. Why did I rent you…

I crossed France just before Christmas. The Eve. I went down the country like a rat hurrying to his hole. It was so dark and. So harrowing to cross these Christmas Eve towns. Their illuminations… Their desert. Their icy squares so empty. A few Happy Christmas bulbs and the darkness.

I still see myself there. The Bear! The Big Bear is there. My chariot of the North…

I see myself on the Christmas road. That road of the Eve of the dead. I see myself old. Older than the Magi. I drove west. Towards my dear mother-in-law's. Towards the countryside. Towards drooling boredom. Towards rustic Sundays. Disembowelled. Stinky.

And then the taste of the cake in your mouth. I will never lose the knack of hating Sundays. God said "It is good", he's resting the Good Lord on the seventh day and men are plunged into Sunday hell.

Twilight, the thrice-reheated coffee, the half-deaf mother-in-law, the damp cake that reminds me of an old sponge. It-is-good… Twilight seeps into the house. Soon the night that opens Sunday. Shutters must be shut – it's my job. I'm going out for my last cigarette. It's my job to announce the night. Day after day… Soft rain, boots and mud… I've got

a spa treatment of sweetish boredom. I want to climb into a cow's arse. To sleep and not to see anything anymore.
The rope, yes. I saw that rope in the barn. Going out for a smoke – I looked at it every night. To hang myself in the barn… It would start to swing slightly. Responding to me. Inviting me, come, come… It saved me that slipknot. It saved me that long dirty rope.

My mother-in-law is getting drunk. My wife is sleeping. Solemnly I was masturbating in the loo. Wait! Careful… No she's asleep. Deeply like a log. Floorboards creaking – mother-in-law doing her rounds… A fat tower of deafness. She passes. Passes… At last she collapses and starts snoring right away – and. If I don't come right now – it won't be possible later on.

I felt old. Greyish days joyless graceless pardonless wordless days. Boots in the morning to go out for a smoke. Stuffing yourself thoroughly until the last gherkin sticks out of your mouth. A little digestive. Some applejack to help you crash down. And so things go by.

Leaving… I was so happy so light! – that I had a hard-on. Ancient Greece-style erection! Joyous! My body was saying farewell to the countryside, farewell to the deaf and hard of hearing. Farewell!

I'm dragging myself. I've become a poor bastard. I say to myself soon soon you will leave here. But nothing is soon. In the best of the worlds – all is well… In hell nothing is soon and hell – it's the countryside. I could have died, sitting like this, my eyes open – never my mother-in-law had interrupted my hours with eyes open. My hours sitting. Never. In the evening she would say – come the dinner is ready… If I wasn't moving she was leaving me alone. I could have croaked… Staying seated in the evenings, at night never bothered me. Certainly not.

When she sees flies crawling all over my mug, in my ears… When she sees them going in and out of my mouth, then yes – she'd notice that I'm dead. That I'm not there anymore. Escaped. She'd be surprised. She'd bury me in her garden. She'd send my wife out on an errand. Far. Her daughter… To spare her… She has guts this old lady! She'd take that heavy square spade. She'd dig deep. A deep hole in a corner. Under Gaston's ramparts. I'd be calm. No more dinners with the deaf.

Holy cow, the bells… The Sunday chapel. It moos the chapel. It turns into a cow. Sunday transforms everything. Street signs I was moving them around, street names, directions – and nothing. Nothing was happening. Nothing was occurring. Not an accident. Not one. Not even a bicycle crushed to a pulp of thick eyeglasses. Not even a worm knocked over! Nothing. Traffic as before as usual. I couldn't see my hands anymore. My open eyes were same as closed. I was really going a bit mad.

My little wife… Scared. Not even existing but scared. To hide. To hide from life. It's easier to hide under a handkerchief in the North Pole.

There is nothing before me. At this sunset party. In this little red tune… The dance of the dead and I – among them. With them. Quiet, the dead. Quiet. We dance and the sun goes away. We dance… So slowly… In a ring. I who loved noon so much. That hour of the dead. The hour when the blood stops flowing.

I'm becoming a shadow… You my son, my swallow what are you singing so softly. You are humming so quietly. You are lulling me… You, my little ruby.
Nothing to catch. Sing this to me… For my old days – sing. Nothing to bring. Souls have no pockets. Tears, go back to where you come from. Beyond this evening I see… the dead. Nothing to grasp. Nothing to hide. A shadow has no pockets.

I have a child and I am not afraid. He is with me and I am not afraid. A man and a child in the city. Alone. Roving… There is something wistful in it. A shadow of a man and a child in a big city. Roving.
Impossible night. Who… Who can find a child in the night… you, night, you've everything. In your arms one can find everything. All the children. Night… Men women. Sad girls. Whores. Everything.
But not a child. Not a day child. You, city, you've everything. Give me my son. You've everything and I've nothing. Nothing! Give me my child back. City… you! You're all the same! All. When it's raining you are all alike. When it's dark you're all the same. Night turns you into Siamese twins. You become one. Yes. One big city. I ask you all. All the cities. I whisper. I know you, night, you don't like racket. Your ear is huge. No screams. Quiet… In the cradle of the night babies are sleeping. Are they quiet… Yes. I plunge into the night like one plunges one's hands into a bucket full of newborn kittens.

To stretch out on the ground and my soul… Let it stretch out too. Give me my son back. I am going out, yes I'm going to come out… Hold me, city. Take my soul. Lose it. But give me my child back. He's only a drop of milk in the night. A tiny little light… City, I will come out into your night.

No child. No child. In the night there's everything, it has all the children but not mine. Not my son. Blackness… Give me my son. Give me my son back, give him back to me white. My drop of milk.

Cities… Empty. Empty… All destroyed. Carcasses of houses. Walls. Bones of cities leaked by the fire. I fly over them. Death isn't home. Above the cities under the sun – I fly. It's so slow… And no one. The sky – a fainted angel's eye.

I am raving I am asking to the Hamlet of my hand – you… My hand – show me – where my son is. To the south of my hand. No. Who then? Who could help me? Not the Hamlet of my hand. Not Lear not the jester… And to the east of my hand – the hunchbacked night of the dawn. My boy, I am raving, son. To the north of my hand – you.

I dive into the night. The diver slowly enters the night ocean… Darkness, take me. I put on my whitest shirt.

To leave here. Leave. To go towards the children. To the parks. Gardens. Towards them… To sit down and. Look from a distance. Not making out their faces. Boys girls. Only that… yes. From a distance. That's all. No faces or voices.

I wear my mother's old kerchief and her smile. When I cross the garden I smile and I feel my mother's face appearing in mine. Her face is coming up in me.

Most seasons I'm on my own. It snows it rains… At Batignolles I wander around, I watch the trains go by. I hear them from a distance, I close my eyes, I listen to them like that. They come closer ta tam ta tam ta tam ta tam they go past and here comes the snow again. I would like to do something, yes something like in my childhood. From this whiteness. A snowman, this kind of thing. I would like to make a snow woman. A woman but there isn't enough snow. Even if I scrape in every corner here – nothing and then they will take me for an idiot. For a meshuggah. Totally!

Their children would come. Hey yippee! We play at making a snowman! They'd all come. Little girls boys... All. They'd come to me enchanted by the snow. Bewitched by the silence. By the silence of my face, by my kind words, by my smile. They'd all come. Yes. All... From all sides of the park they'd come. From the east and the north... From the Cardinet Bridge and from the Avenue de Clichy.

I have to tell them about the bear the snake and the dragon. A little story... The one my son had drawn for me. The dragon, the bear and the snake... Three drawings. I hang them on the wall – the bear, the snake and the dragon. They are above my bed. Above my throat. They protect me.

But I'm careful. I live like a hunting bird. No foolishness, no messing. Children... They are always dragging adults along always. So no foolishness... Keep quiet.

I don't touch your little ones. I don't touch your children. Your cells, I would like to talk to your cells... Am I losing it? Maybe. I don't want to, but not at all, I say to myself – keep quiet. Or else – they'd rip you to shreds. That morbid weirdo, why is he roaming around here? Ugly bastard. Near the kids. Near our little angels. That piece of shit!

And the park would become an evil forest. The forest of angry lambs. Biblical! The Just they'd come in masses, running, you, lambs, in a ring and I, I am alone. You, you are – all, and I – I am alone.

Shh. Not a movement. Look away… Don't look at the children, not by any means. They'd show you your own guts. They wouldn't bother asking you questions… In which dump have you found your dirty eyes? Oh no. They will shut them quick. Shh. Be like a snake.

I didn't touch the children. No. I didn't touch your kids. Monster… I'm not a monster. I didn't do anything to the children. You have to be tender, yes, very tender, yes – and I, I'm dry. I can't I'm scared of people. To be near – no I can't anymore. And children… To be near – no. Their heads, their napes, that smell… No. I am far. I – I am disgust. One has to be tremendous to love this… Your own face in a child.

Snowfall makes us solemn. It feels like a fall in your soul. I heard on TV – it snows in Venice, it snows in Paris, snows falls in the Jura. In Auvergne. Snow covers the Alps. It snows in Burgundy, in the Morvan, in the South. A long snowfall. A man's face lit by fresh snow is the face of a corpse.

The snow is falling. It's heavy. It covers… Here… Everywhere… Let it snow more. Cover everything, snow… Fall more. And more. For days and nights. From morning to evening and more. Let the eiderdown of the sky break. At last… Let it cover it all. And the silence… Faces so pale in the falling snow. So vulnerable… So blind.

Chug-chug chug-chug… Trains are going by, son. Do you remember, we were here, on this bridge, and trains were going by. Going by… We were waving, waving farewell. Trains, people, faces were going by and away forever.

A man and a child on the bridge. To go away, my son. Away… the two of us, to go away. Far away. Not towards the heat… Not the South, son. No. To the North, towards the white. Like iron goes to the magnet, to go away. To take the same road as I had taken once. I know it with my eyes closed. To cross everything… Everything. To turn our backs to Eastern Siberia and – to go up to Yakutia. From Baikal, son, to the Lena. On a ship… Up and up. Through the taiga. Let's start from Lensk. Then Olekminsk. No, surely I'm not mistaken. And then what? Yes – Sinsk. Further up... Sangar. We're getting closer. There, I'm finding my bearings. Those places… Those small towns – I see them like a procession. We slow down… Villages parade, melancholy. Two years, son… In slow motion I see them again. No I'm not sad. Like fish in a shady spot my heart stops.

To go up. Always further up. We pass Zhigansk. Siktiakh… And there – look. We get off near Tiksi.

Let's go. Let the Lena carry us on its back. To the ocean, yes, where it falls into the Glacial Ocean. Where it renders its breath to the Ocean. Where it expires.

The Lonely Island son. There's one, really, it's called like this. No lookout. No more lookouts. The horizon. To look at the ocean until it blinds you. To watch the fjords bare themselves.

It's sleep that kills you in the Great North. You fall asleep and you die. That sleepiness. Leaden lids. And everything will go quiet in the bedlam of my head. At high latitudes. The moon, son… Full like a bucket full of milk in the night.

Let's go Bearcub. Always on the go. Towards something… Far away… Smiling faces, beautiful faces, serious faces. We smiled at trains. We always smile when we see off a train. We wave to those who are on it and smile. A moment… We meet… Too short to hurt… We smile. Too short to become heavy… We smile. We are scared of life and we want to live, son. To live! In this kingdom of shadows we are fish to each other. Not wolf not lion. Fish.

Now I'm alone. Now on this bridge that is so light from all our smiles. Alone I am, son. Heavy I am. It could crash down this bridge. Let the sun go down, too. Let everything go, Bearcub! Everything! No energy to take my hands out of my pockets. Jumping from this bridge, yes, like this, hands in the pockets. Maybe everything, the whole life, my life…was only the road to this bridge. To this leap and then everything would be accomplished? Then everything would be over. Over for good, son?

With me – everything will stop. I'm earth. Like father… I am only your limit, son. You won't go further down, my feather.

Why do I linger here. Why dithering… The ground is so close. From this bridge my whole life I see it. I look at it. A few moments with Babania… A few moments only…

Do you remember Paris, my feather? You came over for the weekend and we stayed in that room, that icy pencil box. We had nowhere to sleep – do you remember, son…

I knew – there were bedbugs and I brought out the mattress – mine – in the corridor. And for you I concocted a nest. A fortress.

And then the pillow fight! Canning you beat me. Pillow blows one, two, oh I can't take it anymore! Have pity… Mercy!

A coup de grâce. You knocked me out laughing… And suddenly – knackered. You yawn. Let's go now…
You fell asleep like a soldier falling in battle but it wasn't the end of it – no. Bedbugs! They came and I saw them coming one by one like at Noah's. The great embarkation.

Those relentless daughters of Arabia. Bugs from all the deserts in the world – not one was missing from the corridor. The silent bugs of Babylon… So big… And even cockroaches. Fat scarabs of Israel. From Ghana, from small Togo, from Libya. From the impenetrable forests of Bwindi.

The light. I leave it on to observe them. Bedbugs. Those old girls… From all the corners of the world. From the bottom of the sky, from the sea, from the deserts.

I have to talk to them. I'm naked – come over here… On me, not on him no – don't touch him. Come. I'm here, lying, I wait for you like a virgin awaiting the sacraments.

My blood. My old – not so rotten my blood. Come on, all-you-can-drink. It's good my blood, get yourself drunk. Drink standing or lying. Get smashed. But him, don't touch him… He's dreaming… His blood is asleep. It isn't a good moment… It's still too young his wine – come on, suck the old one. I have a good flow in my veins… Paint yourself red.
Like the demons Asb'el, Anzû, Asmodai – drink yourself to death. Become my blood brothers. Come on…
The night is yours. Demons from the four corners of the world. Here. Shhh! No screams…

At dawn they will leave this way. Through this window. Down this cliff… Demons on the edge of the night – they will throw themselves down.

Come on – here… My neck. No not here. Lower… Yes. Here it's tender… Good blood. Come on… There's no one. No competition. Quietly. It's night. No one.

To be here… In this misery. A sleeping child and you. You who are offering yourself to the bedbugs as a sacrifice. Who are telling them Feast, it is my blood. You, damaged with neither grace nor magic – soon you'll be old. Really old. You will be reading your old age in the eyes of the others…

I daydream. It's only a dream… A sick dream of a sick man. It's you, yes it's really you who's sick. Your kidneys, you will end up pissing sand. All that… This life Dim… And then we die. And then we don't move anymore. We can't even chase away a fly that tramples our forehead. Life… We should just keep silent. Keep silent and look into the distance.

When we can't take it anymore – we become light, son. And then we fly fly… We get lost. We become lost light.

In the end I will take the road that all men take. Each man. Like a fish that before dying goes back to its birthplace.

Oh our bedbug sojourn! I'm concocting something. I have the patience of a turtle. Little one… I'm going to …

Heavy… I was heavy. But I wanted to be Figaro-like. Light, all feather, all arias. Quicksilver-like. Yes, even when my collar was too tight and the snow was black. But I'm heavy. Sadly heavy. Heavy.

Your life… All that. To tenorise life? To be Boreal of the North or Ariel of the South? – what use would it be?! To aerate the graves? Those beds of the dead? Their beds are empty…

You, my little bear, you didn't have a fairy godmother who watched you sleep. A furtiva lagrima over your cradle – there wasn't any. Shh! Not so loud… Tsss – no noise please. Think less loudly. Your life… It makes an awful racket all that. Your life is laughable… And then your kidneys, you are in pain. Think of something else. A hard-on… Yes, imagine something… Something uplifting, but not that, not your life. Bearcub – it would wake him up…
Do you remember… We danced, you Bearcub, we were waltzing we were Ariel. Ariel… Slowly we were swirling, two feathers.
Your mother was looking at us jealous – oh they're making the cockroaches jump! The dust! Stop! Will you?... Yes my dear yes, there's dust, and we what are we, you I all of us… And when you were glooming, my son – you were asking me to dance for you. You were asking me to tell you what I did when I was little.

My present has no survivors. They are all dead, men, women of my childhood… Dogs too. All, my blood. All. That's why, son – I make the bedbugs dance for you – but not a word about my childhood. You can't pass your hand through the row of my dead. It's a wall, son.
Sleep my little feather, sleep. My eyes are hurting. Terrible particularly in the morning. Drops, all the remedies, tea… And nothing. The doc finds nothing. Tired, Monsieur. Some rest… And nothing. Like my grandmother I'll go blind one day. One night I will wake up blind. In the dark. Blink don't blink – dark.

I'm not telling him about that winter day. I saw a rabid dog for the first time. He was eating snow. We were called in and he was alone on the white. He was crying. He was licking the snow eating it… and then they killed him. From a house yes. Someone – bang! Shot. And once more! He jumped. And then the paws – he moved his paws like he was running when you play at running… He was trying to hide. His muzzle in the snow he was digging the snow to hide yes like he tried to hide… We all saw it. It's short and I'm not telling this to him. I've never told him.

My wife… But seriously. You were saying that I was corrupting my son. That I had stolen his soul… His soul. Stolen… You say all he does is dream of me. My blood. My poor wife. You must have had a hard time… When your son only dreams of the one you despise… My God, you must have copped it old girl. I loved him Son. They say you have to temper that fucking love that dog that toad of love. You have to water it down. To handcuff it. Now I'm going to cage it. Now it's gonna be over. It's gonna be the end caged and muzzled.

My talismans. My son's little things. A straw. His t-shirt. His drawings. There are nights… These things, I look at them. I'm lying and looking at them. These talismans stop the time. The night doesn't move anymore. And I'm suspended in the belly of the night. Hung, these things make the walls bend. The room becomes huge, the walls recede. I understand the dead who come back to see their old room. Our things our places without us or our bodies. Things that strip off our gaze. The dead come back to see their places. Sometimes it makes me sick. To look at these things… My little talismans – it gets me down for days and days. But in the end I will cure my room, I'll manage to heal these walls.

I would like to see their faces… Those three men. Gabriel, Jacky, Georges. They were at the end of their prison term. I first visited them in October. On a beautiful morning, a morning chilly and bright. A deep morning… But after that it was evenings, always evenings.

---Call me Gabriel--- And then he introduced the others. The whole team. It was in Melun.
In the prison. Melun… An old jail. A recycled convent. That island… It's already melancholy in itself. Yes, it's an island. The Seine is sleeping in its bed. I always go there at dusk. From the train, arriving, I saw the street lamps light up. I was going underground in Paris, it was still day, yes, a tired day but a day, and then, when I was getting off in Melun, it was pit night.
I still see myself walking towards that island… It was bathed in a strange light. A halo of black light. Like all the places where men suffer. Like all the places of hardship. Hospitals… All the places of sorrow. I remember the weeping willows and the walls. In the end, I was hearing the walls whisper. That island was whispering to me… Voices of all those hidden people who breathe.
---I Gabriel – twenty-five years of imprisonment for armed robbery---Here's Jacky, twenty years for forgery---Georges… embezzlement… fifteen years of jail---
It was a creative writing workshop. I had gone from one jail to another. Nobody wanted me. In the end I landed up in Melun – that's why I was there. They wanted to write a poem – "When I am not here anymore…" It was their choice.
It will be our testament, Gabriel was saying. He used to be a college principal in Martinique. Ex-principal… In Ford-de-France. He had robbed a bank. With his students…

Armed and all… Three months I spent with them. Three times a week. I had the time…

What does she have to say to me my wife? She reproaches me with Gabie. Gabriel… "But why do you bring everybody home! I'm fed up with it! Fed up, all that misery… Ours, it isn't enough for you!"

But Gabriel isn't everybody. They've come out of hell. Twenty-five years of jail. My big mouth! You might be right my little wife… I'd better shut it. I'm wrong so I am. I'm wrong… They've come out of hell, they did jail time in Burgundy, in Melun, in Montargis and there – in Montargis – it isn't pretty, it's a screws' school and they had to ride shotgun to dodge the nutcases. You're right I don't know them that well, yes not well but to know those who've come out of hell…

We slept in the same room Gabie and I. He had suggested it himself. So self-effacing, he felt your fear.

We have nothing worth stealing and you – you're scared. Do you remember… You used to sing for the old women? In the nursing home… You told me once. You were very beautiful. Do you remember – we walked in the fields at your mother's. You were pregnant. Son… He was on the way. We were travelling miles, we were walking and you were telling me things… You were so beautiful… You told me about those old people before you when you were singing. Where's all that? Where did it go?

You're scared, scared… I, you say that I'm deranged. Crazy because I'm not scared. But no – I am scared. Too. Maybe you're right and I'm sick and… I should head straight to Sainte-Anne, turn myself in, yes.

We went out to play football the three of us. Three men. One who came out of hell, I and Son.

Gabie had nowhere to sleep here in Le Mans. A hotel? Yes. Yes... You're right. Hotel... You can imagine, his permission is about to expire. His children haven't come to see him. It was too tight. And you say – hotel... He was playing football with our son and on the same evening he had to go back to jail.

You have to understand right away. As soon as you are there. In those walls... You are dead. Dead. You come there dead already. The gates close and then – it's over. Over. The silence. In your pockets you still have the smell of the outside but – it's over, the outside. And then it starts. That cold in your balls. Each time each transfer – the same thing.

The silence is full of noises. Shouts. The silence of the dead who scream. Here, nobody hears them – all used to it – except you. You who are a fresh shadow amid the others. It was obvious but there were some who wouldn't understand, didn't want to understand. They were not okay with it at all. Screaming it isn't fair! Why me! I can't believe it... fuck! it couldn't be happening to me! But yes. Yes. They were terribly distressed. They couldn't understand that here – they are only spirits and – you must live in spirit. At each transfer – I saw those guys. They had to change their skin. Each time after a transfer you die and – you change your skin. You are dead again. Just spirits they are. Old spirits. Young spirits. Intelligent spirits. Stingy spirits. Distressed spirits. Gentle spirits. Deranged spirits. Nasty spirits. Angry spirits. Dumb spirits. The body disappears and starts coming back only at night. Comes back with no warning and – you scream. You cry. You pray. You insult all those whom your eyes can see. Eyes of a spirit. Biblical insults – we have loads of them. For years the body comes and goes and in the end – you don't recognise it at all anymore. Used to living like a shadow – you don't look for your body anymore. You don't know it anymore. You forget it. Twenty-five years later I – I look back and I look ahead. I recognise nothing – not people not graves not my dogs not my house. But I don't worry. I don't worry anymore. Spirits, memories, dead… They all enter their kingdom at last…

I lived two lives. And I lived them both to the very end. I was writing to their mouthpieces. That takes some doing. Real love letters. Make them cry! Who nowadays knows how to write to barristers? To judges… That's a different chapter, judges.

You know my road. Twenty years that I've been backpacking. From one jail to another. Here in France, but why not in Martinique? Here I'm freezing when guys are sunbathing. Tell me why not?

It was hot, I remember, hot, bright, splendidly blue and everything started on that day. You know I was teaching literature. Yes… it's been a while. But from here – everything has been a while.

On that beautiful day we robbed a bank. With my former students. Everybody was having a laugh. I wasn't for it. I was laughing. We were just kidding… A bank… They were kids from poor families and life there – I don't need to tell you. Boredom. It bores you rigid the islands. Bores to death. You get drunk. You fight. So the dreams… They were dreaming… And one day they came over in a van. Alright, I say to myself, it's gonna be alright… And then two Kalashnikovs. At that point… I gulped down my burning coffee. It swept me along. It happens that way. Always that way. Just a bit of a laugh… Just kidding and then one day, one fine day – it sweeps you along.

I woke up – I saw two bank employees on the ground. One, I remember – crying… But crying! A guy hulky like a grizzly bear is making my shoes wet.

It was slow. Very slow. I tried to get out of there. Slowly like in a dream. Feet hands… Heavy. Becoming heavy. I was floating… noises, screams, sirens and then – a punch in my nose… and full stop.

Melun. You have to be old I'm telling you and I'd know about it. To survive there you have to become old. To hurry up. To put on a hundred years in one night.

To keep your eyes peeled and to shut them in time. But they, most of them – aren't old enough. Even the hoariest old guys – are too young to live in there. I am not raving I know how you drink in years – in one day. I know the guys there as if I had made them. I gave birth to them. Yes. All. The guys in Melun and that island… Nobody knows my nights, I watched this island this water of the Seine. Nights and nights. I saw the backs of the fish coming up to the surface – on all the sunny days. To catch flies… I saw leaves fall. Gently gliding one after the other. I saw my hair fall…

I'm old, you see. Older than the coast where I was born, older than this rotten island and older that this Seine. Older than your father, your grandfather and great-grandfather… Older than my dead mother and my father. Older than the sand on the beaches there. Far away. Martinique… Martinique… It isn't waiting for me anymore. Even I am not waiting for myself anymore. So old I'll come back and no eyes to recognise me.

They were thinking, a nutcase. Of me, yes, in Melun – here's an old nut. Another one with rats in the attic. Even pals, the oldest ones, they're babies – my old Melun pals. Younger than a foetus. Younger than a stillborn. What am I talking about...

It's a place to suffer with your mouth shut. Each minute – has to be weighed. Each word. Each glance. No one want to say yes to death. Yes – to jail, it is yes – to death. We move there we eat there we wank off there we brush our teeth there we piss we write – and we are dead. All. Screws included. A stiff can do nothing for another stiff. You have to say yes to this. The gates close. We become women in prison. Men – forget and women – remember everything. All those photos, the letters... Little things... We cling to them. We must forget. The gates close and we die and we find ourselves born there. We are born in hell and we live there. But you must forget everything. Purposely... No letters. Nothing. Not a word. Close family the living from the other side will come – but you must be dead for them. Purposely. Particularly for the closest ones. Once, twice – they let you go in the end. All. No one can hold up... To live they need to forget too. To forget you. You die and you go down where the biggest fish are. No need to try catching them – it comes by itself the biggie. Death is just a cloud you have to go through – I say... Let's go now – let's go out. Croissants for you kid. Pittance as you say... Let's go.

Do you remember, Bearcub. You forgot him... Gabriel. Gabie. That old gentleman with glasses that make big eyes. You only saw him for one day. He went away after that. Where? He went far away. He took an airplane, he went to his island. It's very far in the ocean. I received a letter from him. He wrote – *so Dim, so here I am. On my island. Do you remember me? When you haven't seen somebody for ages you never know… Were we first-naming… I'm calling you – Dim…*

I asked you… Once… What were you looking for when you came to Melun? To the prison? To our island… What were you looking for in places like that. In that place of sorrow… And your son… I've forgotten his name. How is he? Does he speak Russian? I am asking you questions. I know you aren't going to write to me. I know it. Jacky wrote to me but it isn't Jacky anymore. It will all crumble in the end. From my house I see youngsters drink and fight on the beach… Every night. Like twenty-five years ago. Lovely sunset. You used to say the best sunset is yesterday's… I often think of these words. You see…

It's hot here. Humid. Trees have grown. I don't recognise anything anymore. Flowers look strange tonight. I'm writing to you because I know that you would like to know the ending. I know that you go to the end of people. To the end of their lives. I'm very old. All my friends have left without waiting for me. And I, I'm tired to stand in this queue. Very tired, friend. I am keen on dying soon…

And a few more words that I didn't understand. Couldn't decipher, and it stays like that.

All our life we search… Someone. Who will live after us. Who at the moment of our death will receive our soul. Someone before whom we won't be ashamed to die. Someone whom you will trust when he whispers – you're dead.

The sadness of the last days. I'm like fish in water in it. I imagine an angel. The angel of the last days. The angel of what we do for the last time. And I see that this angel has no mouth. He says nothing to me. The last day doesn't have a mouth and the last night will be silent. Harvest. The mute angel of the harvests. Yes, I see empty cities. Devastated cities. Cities without us. Carcasses of houses. And I'm flying above… The last day doesn't have a mouth.

Do you remember son, we dropped by to see them in their shop him and his wife. The little Chinese man and his wife. Old, both of them old. They gave you toys… The dragon! Red! It's still alive, no more tail but alive. You don't remember? You fought it in the sandbox. You wrestled in the sand. You were naked. Completely naked! It was hot. Suffocating. That Chinese man mumbling… In tears. Pointing his finger at you and then his wife repeating in French "…hero hero he kills the dragon!..."
They were taking you in their arms. They were touching you. No children of their own. No children.

The woman's eyes were runny. I gave her eye drops but nothing… How are your eyes? It's alright alright… And her eyes were runny. She was laughing. She spoke French a little and he not at all. He was taking you in his arms… Too weak to lift you he was laughing too. He – dry-eyed. They lived a long time. A long time… Two little shadows. And then I hear that they died both of them. With a few months in between. I say – death. Sǐwáng in Chinese. Him first and then her. Shop closed. The House of China it was called. Dust, son. So much dust. Two ghosts, two little ghosts. Do you remember at the back of that shop an alcove. A small altar, a laughing Buddha. Two bowls of rice. Two candles. And the flames.

Death, who can stop you… The elephant stops before the fire. The fire yields to the rain. The tiger backs off before the elephant. Death, who can stop you?... The warrior lingers before the splendid body of a girl. The girl stops before a crying child. The child backs away from his shadow… Sǐwáng! Who can stop you?...

They are blown their candles. The last time – no, I saw them, the little flames. Straight like the souls of that couple. Their spirits went away to the East, towards the yellow dawn. Towards China, son. Two souls lost in the West. Gone. Started the journey to the anthill of the dead. Two smiling shadows, son. They have no one to play with now.

It's noon and I'm dazed. I say – to sell your soul and pay. Dearly… Dearly. To buy a female cat… Let it be a magic one. I would like… An enchanted beast. And to watch her at night. To watch her roam… to watch her turn into a woman. A little woman who jumps into my bed. Who whispers. A female cat who likes drunken men. In the mornings… To see her in the white mountains of sheets – coming towards me.

No more fighting – I say… At the end of all the fights – tenderness. When I muse over this… At the end of hatred – death. Yes. The brightest things are written on black pages. When people, things – everything clears off… the page turns black. The most tragic things are born in the lightness, yes, like a god emerging from dust.

In the throat of hatred – a sick love. A strange lump… A spell "Make me sleep like a drunken goddess who is nodding off…"

I say – the body is a feast. Quietly I rave. I see her… Damiana here. In Paris downstairs in our courtyard. Like a

statue. A statue with hidden wounds. A wounded goddess. If it's possible to wound a goddess…
I see her from here and I'm calm. Very calm. I say that I don't want to die – very calmly – I say… Without getting agitated – I say – I don't want to die… I saw in her what only the dead can see and I say – no… I don't want to die and. I die.
Damiana… She is undressing like a goddess. A goddess coming back from a ball. A witch coming home after a good hunt. I am waiting for her. It was so long… It slows down my blood. She's slowly taking off her feathers. And she smiles.
It is… to close your eyes for… I say – Damiana. Let her be here… Even in spirit but let her be here.
Let her walk around… Three steps to the window and – the sky. She stops for a moment and – looks ahead. The sunset. Then – she looks further out. It's so long. She looks into the distance. Life… She looks looks…
Her face. I'll forget it. Day after day I will be losing her face. My eyes will forget its taste… One day… It will be the end of that face.

I want to be drunk sometimes. To let myself go completely to lose heads and tails. But – I can't. I want to get drunk and fall asleep and – I can't.
Don't turn your head. Stay stay a little longer. Another moment… Like this. Stay the whole life! Let the day die in your eyes. Let it enter you – the vermillion… In the distance – stay. Life… Your eyes in the distance. Let the sky fall. Let it go raving mad with jealousy – stay like this. Don't turn your head. Let everything blow up outside – stay like this. In the distance… Stay like this. Look into the distance. Calm. Ahead.

I whisper and I can't get drunk.
Let her read something Damiana. She's sitting on the mattress. Quietly absorbed sucked in by her book. I'm writing. Yes I'm writing fast I don't stop I'm captured. I don't have the time I'm too close. I don't turn my head… She's there. She's looking at me… From a distance. She was far away in her book. She's coming back.
She smiles. A moment. She doesn't recognise me. She's not from here.

Days… Day after day will pass. Nights. We'll eat at our Chinese around the corner. Sometimes yes, I would want to do the cooking. I would make an effort. The concoction would be good.

She whispers… "Don't look at me. Don't look at me like this. No… Don't take your eyes off me. Look! You smile? I'm drunk, you think I'm drunk! You say to yourself – a drunken virgin… Do you remember you told me – that I'm a drunkard virgin… You said – here's a virgin who took a boozy train running on drunk rails. I remember. Look! Don't look at me. Turn away. If one allows to be looked at this way – one dies. In that gaze. One dies… My grandmother used to say this. We die…"

She whispers at me. And the bed of my soul is empty.

The need of her. Yes, the thirst of her – to be able to go on.

My "Revenants' Ball"… Here… Now. To save my soul. Now. I knew very well that I would need her to be able to write. Need her to be here. In this garret. For her to walk around here, very close, very. Like a big silent bird. They have always inspired me – big birds. To see one very close… I see someone wistful in a big bird. Spellbound.

I say – row… One more oar stroke and you'll be there. Beware of ghosts. A crowd of them here. You live what you scribble.
Write for four hours – and the ghosts turn up. If you stick it out – six hours – it's the female cat that comes. Work for eight hours – and it's the shadows. And if I keep going for nine – it's the dead that I see. My dead. I continue… I work for eleven hours. I'm on all fours. The hour of the spirits… And it's my demons that straddle me. I forget that I'm naked. All day… Towards the end… Shaking from hunger… Like this I gather myself. I keep silent. It's when you fall silent that it begins. You become a witness. A mute witness of your own life. Things people… Everything goes and you remain alone at last.

Before I used to close my eyes to see her. Damiana. Here. In this room. I write this "Revenants' Ball" with my eyes closed.
I won't need to close them anymore. Soon I'll be old. I will grow old alone. I will watch the sun go down. It will go to bed and me too. Soon there won't be anyone to recognise me. Not my son. Not my wife. Not father, not my dead mother.

No one can save me. All those whom I loved become a slipknot for me.

And Damiana… She'll never be here again. I know it with certainty – I will feel a loneliness to summon the dead
---Help! Help me! ---
They can't do anything. The dead… It isn't their kingdom. They will say to me – she isn't here. She. Not one of us.

To save a soul. We are too brittle for it to alight on us. We are only dead branches.
Yes, I would like not to write without her anymore. Without her being here in the room.

I say – lightness… Lightness… It's the only thread that ties distant lovers. Lightness.

I who was game to chop off my foot only to be able to write "At the end of a long long journey the lovers reunite…" If she were here…
A long long journey and at the end – the lovers reunite. This… I will write.

All, yes all… The suicides, the living, the sick, the dead… All – we search. We search for a sorrow… We search for it all our lives. A great sorrow to make us reborn just before we die.

And you you… What are you looking for in those places of sorrow? Houses of pain. Hospitals… Jails. Clinics… Such relentlessness… Who are you looking for? Good for nothing. Good only to pick up corpses with a trolley. To grow them in the basement…
My soul why does it linger around these places?

No not yet… Madness isn't licking my hand. It isn't sucking my cuffs. But why all your life you roam around these places? In search of sorrow.

I say compassion. I will find bodies… Plenty. My mother's. Babania's. My aunt Antonina's. My great-grandfather's… Who would come to claim them? To collect them… Who?

One day… I'll see. While gathering corpses I'll find one. I'll take it into my arms, yes, to see its face. Closer. And I will see it close and I will find peace. Yes. At last.

No one will come to claim this body. No one to bury it. It's me… I will be there to guard it that body. To look at its face. Like one looks at a map of a nearly forgotten country… Left centuries ago… I recognise it little by little. Very slowly. To the end.

I will hide my face in my hands. For a long while. Then I will take it and I will bury it. I will put it into the ground. No matter where. Earth is everywhere. In the end...

The morning star. It shines above the market-place. There... It's the last star. Sirius. The one that dares to stay up so late... I see it from my mattress. Yes it's Sirius and. I see the dogs. They swarm every morning there. They bark and then it's quiet again. All is quiet. Even this killer star. Even Sirius is quiet.
Dogs are devouring cold tripe. Yesterday's tripe. They devour it in silence. They howl sometimes but it's rare. When they fight for a fresh piece. When there're steaming innards. Warm. Then – yes but it's rare.
I would have liked to close my eyes but I couldn't. A curtain... I would have liked a curtain. Let it fall! Let it shut it all out... I would have liked to close my eyes myself. All those days... All that.

To close my eyes. To close them for good. To dream... To make it night and dream.

It's going to be the end. The old souls... They will come into my room. They will all come. They will concoct a funeral meal. And the evening will go by quickly very quickly but I'm in more hurry than the sun. Go away you! Go!!! Go sun... And you, sleep – come.

I see her. More and more often. My crow... It flies, flies my young crow, it flutters around – joyful. I see it from here. In the Paris sky two young crows they flutter, they waltz... They make a pair and dance dance in the sky. When all is over – you will come my crow. From my childhood you will come. From my steppe. You will come specially to show me the way. To my soul you will teach freefall. We'll be a pair.

And it will be light… The fall. Light like a distant song. Like a song that lulls us. At last, I will have something to close my eyes.

How the shadows climb… So gently they slide. So slow… Go away sun! Spill your red and go away. Empty yourself of your red and! Go away. It must stop. Everything. Everything stops. The sun… Leave!

And spirits will come. Souls of the dead… Mine and then others with unknown faces. From the four corners. From far away. They will sing. In no hurry. They are singing now… Yes. An old chant. They are humming it very quietly. It's a lullaby, and let it last… Let them sing. Let it never stop. Their voices sway. Dance. It will be slow. Slow… Through the night and that's all. That's all. Let them never stop. Let it never stop. Voice… Everything started with a voice. All things. All the true movements. And all will end with it. Their chant goes away over the hospital and farther… Beyond the roofs. High… And then too high to follow.

That whole night. And then they fall silent. All. Let it be silent. Let them stop, yes, and at dawn let them shatter my table. And then my bed. Let them shatter my bed. Let them rip my shirt. Break my cup. So that I wouldn't come back again. Dead at last, I will be quite tired quite far away. The ending will be ended and I will never come back again.

Also from Betimes Books

Fionnuala Brennan
The Painter's Women:
Goya in Light and Shade ISBN 978-0-9929674-8-2

Hadley Colt
Permanent Fatal Error ISBN 978-0-9926552-6-6
The Red-Handed League ISBN 978-0-9934331-2-2

Les Edgetron
The Death of Tarpons ISBN 978-0-9934331-4-6

Sam Hawken
La Frontera ISBN 978-0-9926552-2-8

David Hogan
The Last Island ISBN 978-0-9926552-1-1

Kim Hood
They All Fall Down ISBN 978-1-9161565-1-7

Richard Kalich
Central Park West Trilogy ISBN 978-0-9926552-7-3

The Assisted Living Facility Library ISBN 978-0-9934331-9-1

Robert Kalich
David Lazar ISBN 978-1-9161565-0-0

Patricia Ketola
Dirty Pictures ISBN 978-0-9934331-3-9

Jackie Mallon
Silk for the Feed Dogs ISBN 978-0-9926552-0-4

Donald Finnaeus Mayo
Francesca ISBN 978-0-9926552-3-5
The Insider's Guide to Betrayal ISBN 978-0-9934331-6-0

Craig McDonald
One True Sentence ISBN 978-0-9926552-8-0
Forever's Just Pretend ISBN 978-0-9926552-9-7
Toros & Torsos ISBN 978-0-9929674-0-6
Roll the Credits ISBN 978-0-9929674-1-3
The Great Pretender ISBN 978-0-9929674-2-0
The Running Kind ISBN 978-0-9929674-3-7
Head Games ISBN 978-0-9929674-5-1
Print the Legend ISBN 978-0-9929674-7-5
Death in the Face ISBN 978-0-9934331-0-8
Three Chords & the Truth ISBN 978-0-9934331-1-5
Borderland Noir (editor) ISBN 978-0-9929674-9-9

Sean Moncrieff
The Angel of the Streetlamps ISBN 978-0-9929674-6-8

Colin O'Sullivan

Killarney Blues	ISBN 978-0-9926552-4-2
The Starved Lover Sings	ISBN 978-0-9934331-5-3
The Dark Manual	ISBN 978-0-9934331-7-7
My Perfect Cousin	ISBN 978-0-9934331-8-4
Marshmallows	ISBN 978-1-9161565-4-8

Gérard Ramon

In Love with Paris	ISBN 978-2-7466-8421-8

Kevin Stevens

Reach the Shining River	ISBN 978-0-9926552-5-9

Betimes Books, a non-profit literary publisher based in Dublin, Ireland.
For more information please visit www.betimesbooks.com